ONE KNIGHT

THE KNIGHTS OF CAERLEON BOOK 2

INES JOHNSON

THOSE JOHNSON GIRLS

PROLOGUE

Gwin's pulse quickened as she peered down at the disaster before her. Her innate magic tickled her fingertips, eager to get out to bring order to the chaos. Instead, she wrung out her hands and grasped the pointed weapon between her thumb and index finger ready to do battle.

With the quill in hand, the adrenaline rush stole her breath at the loose-leaf sheaths of paper spread across the ancient wood desk. She deftly deciphered the notations and grinned as the data lined up. She made careful notations in the column with her quill. She got a thrill when she found a miscalculation that set the ledger back in balance.

Most girls her age were promenading about the

castle grounds, trying to capture the notice of a knight or squire. Gwin was far more interested in organizing the cupboards or planning the cleaning schedule. She liked order and efficiency.

Even more, she liked that there was always room for improvement. Another pence shaved off the butcher's bill if she chose a different cut of meat for this week's feast. Another second trimmed from the cleaning schedule if they started later in the day to allow an additional hour of sleep.

Blonde hair fell over elegant shoulders as Gwin hunched down, making more markings in the ledger. Her blue eyes hunted for another bit of information that she could bring into order. She was so engrossed in her work, that she nearly missed the voices outside the office door.

"Is there someone in here?" called out a pleasant voice.

There was no fear in the speaker's voice. This was the safest place in the world. Well, that was if you belonged to the community of witches, wizards, and knights who populated the magical town of Camelot. If you were an outsider, then you were in big trouble.

"It's just me, Lady Merylin," Gwin called as the doorknob turned.

Lady Merylin appeared in the doorway of the office of the Lady of the Castle, or the LOC as the townsfolk were fond of calling it. Lady Merylin was advanced in age, but still lovely to behold with her sun-kissed skin, dark hair, and gray eyes so clear it felt as though one could peer directly into her soul. But Lady Merylin's best feature was her smile.

She always looked her best because Lady Merylin always smiled. The expression was like the sun shining. Gwin loved to be in the direct hit of those rays.

Lady Merylin looked around her office space. Her eyes lighted on the neat stacks of books that had been arranged in a balanced tower in the corner. Her gaze shone on the swatches of drapery fabric for the new wing which was now organized by hue. Her brows lifted, casting over the binders on her desk which were now ordered with all sheaths neatly tucked and collated. And finally, that bright gaze dawned on Gwin

"My dear, what are you doing?"

There was a lilting of her voice. That was another thing Gwin liked about the Lady of the Castle. Lady Merylin's voice reminded Gwin of flowers blooming on a spring day.

"I saw that the ledgers needed to be balanced, so

I took care of it," said Gwin. "I also cleaned up a bit and organized a few things. I know you have a lot on your plate with the Choosing Festival, and I wanted to be helpful."

Lady Merylin laughed, a tinkling sound. Gwin had to wonder if it was her smile, her voice, or her laugh that she liked best. It was a very close three-way tie. But then one action triumphed clearly.

Walking toward her, Lady Merylin opened her arms and bundled Gwin up in a hug. This was the best feeling. Hands down.

"My dear girl, you didn't have to do any of this. But I so appreciate that you did."

Over Lady Merylin's shoulder, Gwin spied her mother. Gwynfhar Galahad's lips curled in a rare smile of approval. Gwin's heart swelled even more.

"Although ..." Lady Merylin released Gwin and walked closer to the pile of ledgers on the desk. "It looks like you mixed the Tintagel Castle accounts with the Sterling Castle accounts."

Gwin stepped forward to examine her work and saw the flaw. While Lady Merylin set about rearranging the items, Gwin chanced a second look at her mother. Gwynfhar's smile slammed down. Her mother's crystal blue eyes narrowed into shards of cold ice.

Gwin fastened her gaze to the ground in shame. "I am so sorry, my lady. I'll attend to it straight away."

"Nonsense," said Lady Merylin.

It was even worse than Gwin thought. Now, not only had she lost Lady Merylin's favor, she'd no longer be trusted with any task.

"It's already fixed. And no harm was done," Lady Merylin said in the same cheery voice. Her back was to Gwin and her mother so she didn't see their exchange. When Lady Merylin turned, her smile was as bright and welcoming as ever. "I truly appreciate that you did this for me. It was so thoughtful."

Lady Merylin gave Gwin an affectionate pat on her shoulder. It wasn't a hug, but it was still nice.

"Now, that's enough of you doing chores for the day," said the elder woman. "Go out and enjoy the festivities. I insist."

"Yes, my lady." Gwin bobbed a curtsy and turned on her heel.

She avoided her mother's gaze as she walked past her. Gwynfhar had already plastered on what Gwin's younger sister, Morgan, called the Hostess Smile. The smile was an even lift at both corners of the mouth to show balance. A slight gap broke the middle of the mouth for a flash of white to show ease. And the head dipped down slightly to show deference.

It was a look Gwin had yet to master. Her feelings were always on her face. Gwin shut the door to the LOC office behind her and sagged against it. Both her body and her face dipped low.

"Is it safe to come out?"

Gwin looked up to find her sister slinking around a corner. Morgan was dressed in a corset-less dress that came above the ankles. She did it because it was easier to move when she did her experiments, and only while inside the castle walls, but it was still scandalous.

"Mother and Lady Merylin are in there. Oh, Morgan, I made a mess of things. I combined two different ledgers."

Morgan nodded, her brow furloughing as she did so. Gwin waited for her sister's consoling words, but Morgan looked as though she were waiting for Gwin to say more.

"Is that all?" Morgan asked.

That was enough. Gwin was used to being of assistance and being an aide in whatever she did. She was called on as a healer due to her unique magic, and she relished the opportunity to help others. She wasn't used to doing harm.

"Well, at least you didn't blow up the barn."

"Oh, Morgan. You didn't."

"I was testing out this new gunpowder chemical my friend, Alfred Noble, came up with. You remember we met him last year in Sweden? Anyway, he had the brilliant idea to mix nitroglycerin with clay and sodium."

Morgan's eyes were alight with excitement. Gwin couldn't help a small smile when her sister spoke about her true passion, which was the field of science. But the practical part of Gwin had to ask. "What of the barn?"

"It's still intact. Well, the roof is. But one of the walls has a bit of a hole. I was repairing it myself when the Authoritarian stormed in."

Gwin shook her head solemnly. "It's mother you should be worried about. She still has her mind set on you and Arthur forming a match."

"Oh, no," Morgan said in a flat voice. She put her hand to her head and fluttered her lashes. "Do you think I've ruined my chances?" Morgan dropped the damsel act and pulled a sickly green look over her features. "Not everyone wants to get married and organize a home."

"Is it wrong to want to be a good and useful person?"

"You know, I've been reading the writings of a psychologist."

"A what?" asked Gwin.

"Psychology. It's the study of the human mind. This German man, Freud is his name, he believes that all of our adult problems are a result of our personal development which is determined in early childhood. So, in effect, anything we do wrong is mother's fault. I find that not only exacting but a relief."

"Mother only wants what's best for us, Morgan."

"Marrying an invalid old man is not what's best for you, Gwin."

"Merlin isn't old. Not by magical standards. He's in his prime."

"He's sickly and frail, and he only wants to marry you because he needs your magic to heal him."

"What do you think I should do?" asked Gwin. "Keep my magic to myself? Be selfish? If I can be of help then, it's my duty to do so."

"I'm never getting married." Morgan's body shuddered at the mere thought.

"You say that now," Gwin chided.

"I'll say it a hundred years from now, too," Morgan called over her shoulder as she scurried off.

Gwin watched her sister disappear down the

hall. Unlike the human women of this time period, witches were now and had always been fiercely independent creatures. But not so independent as to eschew the idea of a lifelong partner and children.

Marriage and motherhood had long been a dream of Gwin's. She hadn't grown up idealizing matrimony as most women in the town did. She knew it to be what it was; a practical union to strengthen the community. She had a healthy respect for the institution of marriage and was eager to embrace her role as head of her household, or better yet, Lady of the Castle. The role would someday be hers.

Gwin pressed her hand to the office door. One day, she would have the run of it. But for now, she did as Lady Merylin bade and headed out to the festivities. A good LOC was more than an organizer. She was also a consummate hostess.

Outside Tintagel Castle, in the fields used for jousting and squire training, the knights were putting their sons, nephews, and distant cousins through the paces. The time had come for many of the magical swords of the Knights of Camelot to choose their new masters.

The first person Gwin saw when she came toward the field was her betrothed; Merlin. The elder son of Lord Arthur, the second of his name, sat beneath a parasol. His lanky body was hunched over as he coughed into a piece of linen watching the activity of the men out on the field.

Just a few months ago, Excalibur had chosen Sir Arthur, the third of his name and Merlin's younger brother, to wield it. It wasn't uncommon for a sword to skip the first son, or to even choose a distant relative. The line of succession was entirely the will of the blade.

There were many men on the field hoping to be chosen as the next generation of knights. Gwin knew most of the faces. She saw the two sons of Sir Geraint. Sir Geraint's youngest son chatted with the son of Sir Gawain. The two were likely planning mischief. Sir Tristan's little boy trailed behind the two older knights in his role as squire.

And then Gwin spotted someone new.

She would not have noticed him except his hair. It was such a vivid and bold color of red that it invited the eyes to stare. And stare she did. At more than just his hair.

Gwin had seen many fine men in the town; knights, warriors, even princes, and kings came to visit. Many were handsome and well-put together. But there was something different about this boy, no man. His shoulders looked broader than any others. His forearms looked more muscled; his chin more square.

She spied powerful thighs at the edge of his plaid. Thick, bulging muscles that rivaled a horse's flank. She wondered what it would feel like to mount and ride his rump.

Her cheeks reddened at her lewd thoughts. Such an idea had never once entered her mind. Gwin lifted her gaze and met his eyes.

Such a shock of blue that she'd only seen one time before... on the face of Sir Lancelot, the second of his name.

Perhaps this young man was a distant cousin? If so, Gwin wondered why she'd never seen him before? Sir Lancelot had no sons of his own, and would likely not have any anytime soon. His dear wife had been in sickbed for much of the last decade with a disease that Gwin's magic couldn't heal.

Gwin continued gazing into the red-headed man's blue eyes until she realized, the reason she saw them so clearly was because he was staring back at her. Embarrassment stormed over her, but she couldn't look away. It was as though his eyes held her in place. He smiled at her like no man had ever smiled.

Gwin's cheeks heated. The heat broke the spell, and Gwin gasped. Was he a wizard?

Gwin shrank back into the woods. She should've gone to Merlin, to see if her fiancé needed any tending, but he had color in his cheeks today. And it looked like it was only a minor cough. If he needed her, he'd certainly say so. Loud and clear enough for everyone to hear it and send someone to find her.

That was mean of her. She didn't begrudge Merlin. She didn't know what it was like to be ill. It had to be hard for him.

She knew he wanted to be strong and able like his father and younger brother. It was a blow to Merlin when Excalibur chose Arthur. But Merlin's magic wracked his body far too much for him to lift a sword most days.

They'd discovered that Gwin's magic soothed the savage magic inside him. They'd discovered this when she'd come over to him as a child and touched him. She and Merlin had been in each other's company ever since. It was inevitable that they would get married.

She cared very much for Merlin. She was sure that care would turn to love one day. Perhaps not blinding and all-consuming passion as other ladies spoke of or what she read in novels. What she had with Merlin was familiar. And it was nice to be needed and appreciated and-

"Oof!"

Gwin tripped over a tree root having not looked at where she was going. The hem of her dress got tangled, and she couldn't maintain her balance. There was no time to cast a spell to right herself. She was falling to the ground. Gwin reached out her hands to protect herself. But there was no impact.

She was caught in a hug. A hug that was warmer than Lady Merylin's. A tight embrace that made her feel safe and secure. Gwin's instinct was to cling to this feeling and stay in the space forever.

"Are you all right, lass?"

The deep voice startled Gwin. She lifted her hands and shot witch fire. The red-haired boy took a direct hit on his arm and went down. She also went down as he had been holding her, keeping her from falling.

Gwin scrambled to her knees and crawled over to him. "I'm so sorry," she said when she reached him. "You startled me."

His eyes were closed. They opened slowly, focusing on her. She had the occasion to watch that unique blue clear and come into focus. She felt like she was watching magic unfold.

Gwin felt something ignite down in the depths of her soul, deep in her gut where her magic lived. Her heartbeat sped up, pounding against her chest cavity so loudly that it rattled her rib cage. Her mouth filled with desire, and she had to swallow it down once, twice. Even with her throat clear, she still couldn't find her voice.

"Hello," he said.

"Hello," she said.

They continued to stare, blue eyes latched on blue. Gwin didn't understand the fog happening in her head. She felt as though magnets were growing between them. Not the polar opposite charges Morgan had shown her. It felt like they were the same charge fighting to get closer and make a connection.

"Are you a wizard?" she asked.

He smiled and it dazzled her. "No. I'm a bastard."

Gwin gasped at the use of the foul language. "That's not a proper word."

"My apologies," his Scottish accent was thick on his tongue. "I suppose I shouldn't say that to a lady. But I have not been around many ladies to know better. Still, that improper word is what I am. My father lay with my mother while he was wed to another."

She knew such things happened, but not often in Camelot. His father must be of a line that lived outside a magical town that was on the ley lines that spanned the world.

Though his birth was dubious, that made him no less of an equal. At least not in her view. Her mother would definitely believe differently.

"The circumstances of your birth do not dictate the path of your life," she said to him. "Only you can do that."

He stared at her for a moment before saying, "Here, let me help you up."

She hadn't noticed that they were both still crouched down on the ground. She was leaning over him as he lay on his back. The position wasn't proper, but it had felt so right being this near him that Gwin hadn't noticed the impropriety.

Gwin straightened, coming first to her knees. The young man made to sit up but winced. There was a red mark on his arm where her witch fire had hit him.

"I'm so sorry," she said. "I can heal that."

She reached out to his arm. She pulled from the well of magic that lived inside of her. There was plenty of herself to give, she didn't need to tap into the ley energy that ran beneath the entire town.

His face lit in wonder as he watched her. His eyes stayed fastened on her face, not on what she was doing. Warmth flooded her as she touched his skin. She didn't want to pull away from the sensation. She wanted to get closer to it.

"Do you feel that?" he asked.

"Feel what?" But she knew exactly what he was talking about. As she pulled on her magic, something else pushed its way into her being. The sensation pooled in her heart.

"It feels like the world coming into focus and making sense for the first time." His eyes dipped to her lips.

It was like a tale out of a fairy story or a romance novel. It was what she'd always imagined falling in love would feel like. The moment was so ripe for a kiss. And then it all fell apart.

"You bastard."

One moment, Gwin had seen her life laid out before her. So clear, so perfect, so right. The next moment, that feeling was yanked away from her as the man, whose name she still didn't know, was wrenched from her.

It was the worst feeling, having her destiny stripped from her. Gwin looked up to see Sir

Lancelot. His face inflamed a deeper shade of red than his hair.

"I knew I shouldn't have brought you here, you ingrate." Sir Lancelot was so angry that spittle collected at the sides of his mouth.

The young man who was his mirror image from younger days scrambled to his feet. His head had been high, even when he'd called himself that foul word. Now it hung low at hearing it hurled from another. "Nothing happened father-"

"Don't you dare call me that. You're nothing but a by-blow. And now I catch you taking advantage of a lady."

"He didn't take advantage," said Gwin. "He was wounded. I was healing him."

"He's beneath your notice, my lady," said Sir Lancelot. "If I could smite out his existence with this sword, I would"

Sir Lancelot raised the blade as though to strike. The young man didn't cower. He stood tall and proud, ready to take his punishment. But Sir Lancelot was having trouble moving the sword.

The elder knight's eyes widened, going from his son to the sword. Sir Lancelot struggled as though he were trying to hang on to the blade, not slice it downward.

"No," growled Sir Lancelot, now using both hands to hang onto his blade. "Not him."

The sword didn't listen to its former master; as magical swords were wont to do when their former master's time was up. The sword slipped from Sir Lancelot's grip and hovered before his son.

1

a century later...

There was something satisfying about the clashing of swords. The blades made a ringing noise which sounded to Lancelot like chimes. It was musical really, especially when the opponent was a practiced artist of swordplay.

Lance's last opponent had made a terrible gnashing sound with his blade as he struck down like the amateur that he was. The sound so offended Lance's ears that he'd quickly dispatched the man and the poor, unpracticed lump was now lying still on the floor, a mortal wound leaching his life from him.

This current swordsman made a better sound with his weapon. Instead of constant overhaul strikes like a mallet hitting a gong, the man had some skill with his upward strikes, parries, and ripostes. But all of his rigor made it clear to Lance that the man was trained in the pretty dance of fencing.

Even worse, the man had obviously learned sword fighting from a dainty French teacher. Most of the modern day order of the Knights Templar received such instruction. It was a tradition that was unsustainable, especially against a brawler born in the Highlands like Lance.

Loren, Dame Galahad, was fond of calling Lance the Highlander after a movie series of sword-carrying immortals who fought to the death with long blades. A fencer's foil was a fool's weapon. Their technique was no match for him. Loren was the only fencer who could meet his metal. This man was no Loren.

The man's sword clashing against Lance's did make for some interesting music, however. The melody of the Templar's thin blade to Lance's thick steel was pleasant to Lance's ear. Too bad it was clear that by the crescendo of this particular song that his opponent would not win.

Lance easily got under the man's defense with his blade. Secace, the sword of the Lancelots ripped open the Templar's traditional white tunic. Blood seeped from the red cross over the man's shirt exposing the man's bird-like chest.

The Templar looked down at his ruined wardrobe and skin. He glared up at Lance. "You bastard."

A tick started in Lance's eye. His jaw ground. He rolled his neck, but he couldn't shake the sound of his father's voice in his head. "Don't much like that word."

Once upon a time in his life, Lance hadn't minded it. It was technically what he was after all; a child born out of wedlock. But the circumstances of his birth didn't dictate the path of his life. Since learning that wise lesson, he'd been determined to become the most devout man, the most chivalric knight in history. And he'd succeeded.

"It'll be the last word you hear, bastard."

Secace positively vibrated in Lance's grasp. The magical sword didn't take to the word either. The moment Lance's father had hurled it at him over a century ago, the sword had left the elder Lancelot and chosen the illegitimate son.

The Templar's blade clashed again with Secace.

The battle hymn was approaching its final note. Unfortunately, the sound of the Templar's blade struck a wrong note. With a kick to the solar plexus, Lance knocked the man off balance. Then with a pirouette, the only French move in his arsenal, he brought down his sword. Blood splattered, playing the final notes of this death march.

"Lance, stop dicking around," called Percival. "We've got a quest to complete."

Lance turned to find the dark knight peering out of a room in the Templar's not-so-well-hidden bungalow. They'd managed to sneak into the Templar hideout virtually undetected.

Templars were the sworn enemies of the Knights of Camelot. The order believed witches were the children of Eve and the Devil—a result of the Devil's temptation from when Eve ate the apple. They believed all witches and wizards were set on seducing humanity to the dregs of evil.

Witches were some of the most beautiful women of creation. They could be seductive to get their way. However, they lived by the same chivalric code as knights. Most of them, anyway.

There was some truth to the story of the forbidden fruit from a tree. But the Templars' version was largely out of context. And besides, God never condemned Eve. It was Her work that the knights were doing—keeping magic out of the hands of erratic humans.

The Templars were determined to capture and destroy anything magical. That included books, artifacts, and magical beings. Lance pulled his sword from the downed Templar's stiff body.

Though Lance had quickly dispatched of these two Templars, he hadn't done it quietly. He felt others stirring above. He and Percy might have to confront the cavalry soon. If the backup brigade was on par with the advanced guard, Lance didn't give a care.

He walked into the room where Percy sat at a computer console. Lance barred the door behind him. Then he turned and did an inventory of the space.

The room reminded him of the Weapons Room back home. The sanctuary of the knights and squires sat just above the dungeons of Tintagel Castle. Here, in the enemy lair, were swords and other medieval weaponry on the walls. Templar robes hung on a rack in one corner next to business suits and jeans.

Were these men part-time fighters? Lance felt insulted. His entire life was devoted to the cause.

In another corner, there was a window. Looking out, Lance saw it led to a wooded area. As Percy clacked on the computer, Lance checked the latch of the window. It gave easily. There were bars at the window, but they were nothing to a magical sword with a supernaturally sharp blade. Escape would be easy.

"Malegant's long gone," said Percy when Lance came to join him over the computer console. "Those were just the second string out there."

"More like third string," grumbled Lance. He'd been itching for some action for days. He had a lot of pent up energy that needed somewhere to go. The pursuit of Camelot's newest villain was the perfect outlet.

Malegant was the latest Templar leader to rise through the waning ranks of the crippled order. Only a year ago, Lance and his brethren had dispensed of the senior leadership, cut off their source of income, and seized much of their land. Only small pockets like Malegant's existed any longer.

Unlike the Knights of Camelot who were born to the station, new Templars could be recruited and trained. Though poorly.

The knights had Malegant's son, Simon Accolon,

in their possession back in the dungeons of Tintagel. Accolon was a physicist who had been working on discovering new elements on the Periodic Table. He hadn't discovered one. Lady Morgan had. That element was the core of magic.

Accolon had tried to steal the element from Morgan. He'd nearly succeeded before Arthur took him down. And now the scientist was spilling all that he knew about his father's plans.

Percy, the computer wiz of the knights, had tracked Malegant to this bungalow in Tripoli. Tripoli was one of the last Crusader states. There were ancient scrolls, an arsenal of vintage weapons, and even miles of mysterious concoctions throughout this hideout. But the Templars had touched none of these. Left on the ancient desk was a modern computer with no passcode locking the screen.

"Malegant must have known we were coming and fled," said Lance.

"Without taking or even locking his computer?" Percy scoffed. "It's too convenient. It's as though he wants us to follow him."

"Have you found anything that might indicate where he's heading next?"

"There's just more gibberish about the stone army."

It sounded like gibberish, but Lance knew better than to discount it. He'd seen flowers raise their heads and blink their stamen eyes. He'd seen dragons take to the sky. He knew that in Greece, Loren and her BFF Dr. Nia Rivers had battled a Titan god who'd risen from a stony grave.

Lance lived amongst witches and wizards. A spell to animate stones wasn't too farfetched. A Templar resorting to magic, however, was baffling.

There was a commotion outside the door. It seemed the new recruits of the Templars had found their hidey hole. Both Lance and Percy ignored the banging and puzzled over the information on the computer screen.

"He seems to be retracing the steps of the Grand Masters of the Knights Templar. Jacques de Molay spent a lot of his time here in the East Outremer."

The Outremer literally translated to "overseas" in French. It included the territories of Crusader states, principalities, and lands taken during the First Crusade. Tripoli in northern Lebanon was one such Outremer.

"De Molay was the last Grand Master," said Percy. "But there's also notes about the first."

"You mean Hugo de Payens?"

De Payens was a name all of Camelot knew. He

was a descendant of the first family of Camelot. He'd betrayed the knights and broken the alliance between the original Templars and Camelot.

"The last entry makes reference to Champagne," said Percy.

Lance knew Percy wasn't talking about the beverage. He meant the region in France; another important place in history for the Knights of Camelot and the Knights Templar alike.

"Let's take this information back to Camelot, see if we can make some sense of it."

Both Lance and Percy's heads lifted as the banging on the door increased.

"Looks like we're done here." Percy shut down the device and looked to the window. "Shall we make our escape?"

Lance pressed his thumb on the rounded pommel of his sword. The magical blade retracted and folded itself into a Cairngorm brooch, trading the cold steel gray for the brown rock crystal of the mountains where he was born. All magical swords were able to shift their shapes so that the knights could hide their magic in plain sight in these modern times.

Arthur's sword, Excalibur, transformed into a pen. Loren's sword, which she'd renamed Inigo after some film, had hidden itself from her as a cane until she claimed her family's seat. Though Lance no longer wore a plaid, he pinned his sword to his shirt at the fabric near his chest.

"And look, this will be a first," said Percy. "You didn't get wounded."

"Of course, I didn't. Those amateurs aren't worth my blade." Lance walked toward the window. Through the glass, the forest was free and clear.

"That means there's no need to visit the infirmary."

Lance's hand froze on the latch to the window. His gripped tightened on the loose handle. "It won't budge. Looks like we'll have to fight our way out."

"Hmmm." Percy twisted his lips. "Imagine that."

Lance pulled the brooch from his shirt. Instead of meeting the other knight's gaze, he pressed the center gem that would release his blade. He went to the door and opened it. The last thing he heard before the battle cries of ten Templars was Percy's muttered curse.

"And they say I'm the crazy one," came the grumbled complaint of Percy before he too rushed into the fray.

2

Gwin felt her heart beating in her fingertips. Her hands were empty, palms sweaty as she faced this big decision, a decision that would impact the future of all of the residents of Camelot for generations to come.

Her choice blared brightly in front of her eyes. Her two options flashed, urging her to decide.

Did she want to update to the newest version of Windows? Yes, or No?

It was a major decision in the realm of file management. Stick with the tried and true? Or risk the brave new version?

She hit the Yes button. Without risk, there was no reward.

Gwin wasn't known for her risky or risqué

behaviors. Since becoming Lady of the Castle nearly a century ago, she'd toed the line, stayed on track, kept her hands clean, and did her duty. Just as she'd been raised to by her mother, trained to do by Lady Merylin, and expected to do by all of the people of the town.

The screen flashed blue. When it blinked back on, all that remained was a status bar. It read 1% complete. It estimated its task would not be finished for two hours.

Gwin tapped her fingers on the desk. All was orderly on the tabletop. She'd finished putting the castle's ledgers in order. She'd placed all the orders for the month. The printer had already printed the last report before she started the update.

Though she lived in the modern age, she still liked to keep with some of the old ways. Lady Merylin had written everything down by hand. Gwin preferred the printed word to her own handwriting. She placed her sheets in the ledger alongside Lady Merylin's old binders. Hundreds of years of order were all in alignment.

Gwin sighed and pushed back from the desk. Her work here was nearly done. Soon, her sister would take over and Gwin would be free to ...

Well, she didn't know exactly what she'd do. But

she did know there was plenty left to do. And there was no time like the present to get started.

Gwin waved her hand in the air. Magic flowed from her fingertips and pushed the pages in the ledgers a smidge until they were all in perfect alignment. With everything in order, she marched purposefully to the door of her office. She was uncertain of which direction she'd turn on the other side, but she'd cross that bridge once she crossed the threshold. Before she reached the threshold, the office door crashed open. Her sister slammed the door behind herself and then slumped against the closed frame.

"Morgan?" Gwin reached out to her sister, prepared to heal whatever ailed her.

"Save me," said Morgan.

There wasn't a scratch on Morgan or her graphic T-shirt. No bruise on her exposed olive skin. No tears in her blue eyes.

"Let me guess," said Gwin. "Wedding planning?"

"It's like I'm walking in a real, live nightmare. Like my real-life is literally a bad dream." Morgan turned the lock on Gwin's office door before coming deeper inside to slump in the chair in front of the desk.

Gwin tried to hide a smile but failed. Her baby

sister was getting married. The man hadn't been the one of Morgan's dreams. But that was only because Morgan had never dreamed of getting married. Love never worked out as one planned it. Gwin knew that better than anyone.

"There are fittings and tastings," Morgan moaned. "I'm being asked about the silverware. What do I care about the silverware? We can eat off of paper plates and plastic, reusable forks. It would be better for the environment."

Gwin winced. "I hope you didn't say that suggestion out loud."

"You'd think I'd asked to have an orgy at my wedding with their reaction."

Pretty much. With the old biddies of the town, it was a sacrilege request. Though Camelot existed in the modern day, there were some things that were simply traditional in this ancient town filled with people from the Dark Ages to the Enlightenment and the Industrial Age.

"I wish Arthur and I could just elope," Morgan sighed.

"Morgan, don't you dare." Gwin came over and perched on the edge of her desk. "The whole town is looking forward to this celebration."

"The town can have the wedding. I just want my

relationship with my man. I didn't realize how much I'd be signing up for when I agreed to marry him."

Gwin squeezed her sister's shoulder. Morgan was as tense as a rock. "I'll be here to help. Not with the marriage obviously. But with the wedding and all your duties after."

"Gwin, we already talked about this. You'll still be LOC. You're still married to the eldest Pendragon, and even when he passes away, the role will still be yours."

"That's not tradition."

Gwin had been married to Merlin for years after his father died. It wasn't until the passing of Lady Merylin that Gwin picked up the mantle of LOC, though she'd been doing the job for years.

"Nothing like this has ever happened before with the Lord of Camelot turning evil. Well, not unless you count Hugo de Payens. But he wasn't in line for the Lordship. We're making it up now, and what *we* want matters."

Gwin decided not to argue. It was wisest not to fight with a bride before her wedding. Gwin had never argued as a bride. Not during her engagement to Merlin. Not during her marriage. Not now, as her ailing husband-turned-notorious-villain lay dying.

She'd always done what was asked of her. She

often went above and beyond. Because that's what she was called to do. Her duty.

Duty would dictate that she comfort her sister. Duty would insist that Gwin go and see to her husband; the man who had caused utter devastation on the town last year.

She'd do it not out of love. She'd never loved Merlin. Not in the way she knew that other couples loved. She hadn't been taught what that kind of love was, not until it was too late.

She knew there were other types of love. There was the familial love that she showed to her parents and relatives. There was sisterly love that she showed to Morgan and to their cousin, Loren, who was like a sister to them both. There was love of community that she doled out in spades to the people of her town.

And there was love of duty. That is what she reserved for Merlin. It was her duty to tend to her husband. There was no one else to perform the task as he transitioned.

The other type of love, the romantic type, the all-consuming type, the type that kept you up at night with fevered dreams that made your undergarments damp with want type. Well, that type was not for Gwin. Her heart was filled enough with the myriad of other ways and other people that she welcomed into her big heart.

"Come on." Gwin ushered Morgan up and toward the door. "Let's go and choose some silverware."

Morgan groaned, but she allowed herself to be dragged.

This was a good sign. If Morgan didn't truly want to do something, she could not be moved. The bride to be slumped into her sister as they trudged down the hall toward the stairs that led to the Great Hall.

"What if," said Gwin, "instead of silver, we chose a different metal from the Periodic Table of Elements."

That piqued Morgan's interest.

"What about nickel or zinc?"

Before Morgan could answer, a commotion sounded in the Throne Room. The two sisters looked to one another and then hurried down the grand staircase. In an unladylike fashion that would give their mother palpitations.

Gwin knew that there had been a quest this morning. Morgan had been the one to send Lance and Percy off while Gwin had tended to her duties. It sounded like they were back now.

Gwin felt the burst of energy from the ley line as

she rushed through the entryway of the Throne Room.

Her feet pumped to a stop before going too far. Arthur didn't like witches to come into potential harm. Morgan kept going until she was at her betrothed's back. Arthur scowled at her before encasing her in the protection of his arms.

Constance Bors opened the ley line doorway and Percy and Lance rushed in. Percy walked through untouched, but there was a gash on Lance's shoulder.

Gwin gasped at the sight. She lived in a castle filled with knights and squires. The sight of blood was a common enough occurrence. But any time that blood was from Sir Lancelot, her heartbeat tapped out a specific pattern.

Lance looked up at the sound of her gasp. Their eyes caught and held. And held.

"Go get that looked at in the infirmary." Arthur's voice boomed loud enough to break Lance and Gwin's gaze. "We can debrief after you're healed."

"I'll help," said Lady Constance. She reached out to Lance, touching his injured shoulder carefully.

Lance's jaw tensed at her touch. He looked down. Disappointment clear on his face.

"Actually, Lady Constance," said Morgan, "I was

hoping you would help me with some wedding details? I hear you have excellent taste in silverware."

Gwin could've kissed her sister. By the look he gave her, Lance felt the same about Morgan's interference.

"I can see to Sir Lancelot," said Gwin. "And I can do it here. No need to go to the infirmary."

The same infirmary where her husband lay clinging by his grasping hands to life. No, there was no need to take the man who held her heart in there. The room cleared until there was only Lance and Gwin left.

3

───────

The sun tracked her like always. Lance had been to many theatrical showings in his lifetime. He had an affinity for musicals, poetry, and things that sounded pleasing to the ear. In these productions, light always shone brightest on the star of the show. Spotlights, floodlights, backlights painted the stages with illumination.

Nothing held a candle to her.

The sun shone differently when its rays touched her. The particles looked bigger, brighter. They twinkled in the air around her as they fell from the sky.

The first time Lance had seen Gwin, the sun had framed her. He'd been looking for a wayward arrow. He'd been lead straight to her. Everything always came back to her.

She was a rainbow shining brightly after a storm. The treasure his heart sought to make his life worth living. And, like a rainbow's treasure, she was always just beyond reach.

Gwin came closer. Her rays warmed him through. Lance closed his eyes and basked in the warmth he could never touch.

"Are you in pain?" she asked him.

Every day I cannot kiss you. "It's manageable."

He opened his eyes. Their gazes connected. Had she heard his inner yearning? At times, he was sure she did. But he'd been sure that first moment a century ago, when his heart took its last beat on its on just before saying, *That's her.*

From then, his heart beat solely for Gwin. Had room only for Gwin. Broke when Gwin made vows to that sickly sycophant.

Lance was not in attendance on that fateful day. Up until her wedding day, they hadn't had another moment alone again. He had been whisked up into his new duties as a knight. He'd become distracted by the new friends he'd made in the other initiates.

Still, she was never far from his mind, though she remained entirely out of his reach.

It was laughable. His father, in particular, had

laughed a lot. A genteel lady and an illegitimate bastard?

Stranger things had happened, like that same bastard finding his deadbeat dad, learning he was from magical royalty, and then being named heir all in the same week.

Lance vowed he'd make himself worthy of Gwin. He pledged that his heart would only ever be hers. He committed his mind, body, and soul to the pursuit of her happiness and well-being. As he made these solemn promises, she made vows to another.

Another man would've freed himself from such an untenuous situation. Not Lance. Lance took vows seriously, likely because his life was the result of a man's broken vow.

He kept the promise he'd made in his heart to his lady. He made it formal on the day she bound herself to another. Lance's devotion to Lady Gwin was unconditional, noble, and pure.

His love for his lady was morally beyond reproach. It was transcendentally beyond the human or magical experience. It was physically a swift and accurate kick to the blue brooches between his legs each time he beheld what he could not behold on the arm of the undeserving ingrate that was her husband.

"I can make it better," Gwin said.

Lance had forgotten about the pain in his arm from his encounter with the Templars. One had gotten in a lucky riposte. Or Lance had lowered his guard to allow the flesh wound. Or whatever.

Offering Gwin his arm, he wondered if she could see his heart pound out of his chest to get to her? Surely she could feel his pulse race as the pad of her thumb hit his skin. He tried and failed to divert his gaze from her. It was so rare that he was this close to his heart's desire.

He was so alert, so attuned, that he had long ago memorized the grooves of her fingerprint. He knew without looking that her more narrow index finger wrapped around his bicep. She didn't land the last four in order. He felt her pinkie, then her middle finger. Last was her ring finger. As always, she was careful not to let the band touch his skin.

It was enough.

Lance took what he could get of her. He'd lived his life as a thirsty man in the desert for a century. He was joyful of each drop and savored it. Each taste made his exile bearable.

"You're the greatest warrior in Camelot next to Uther Pendragon, but you keep getting hurt." Her smile teased as her fingers held him. "Didn't they teach you to avoid the sharp end of the sword in knight school?"

He would take a thousand lashes for a few stolen moments such as these. "It's just a scratch, milady. Not truly worth the gift of your magic."

Gwin lifted her gaze. Her clear blue eyes told him she knew he didn't mean those words. They both knew she lived for these healing moments as much as he did. The sessions soothed more than Lance's surface wounds. Longing gazes and furtive touches were all that were allowed of them.

It was enough.

Just as when they first met, a whole conversation played out between them in the blink of an eye. These conversations always began the same with those long, soul-searching gazes. It was the most comfortable, natural thing to gaze into Gwin's eyes. She allowed him to see into her soul.

In the chatty silence, Lance checked for cues of her health in the whiteness of her gaze. He peered down at the amount of darkness in the circles beneath her eyes. He inspected the lift of her brow to tell him whether she was in good spirits this day. The pull of her lips told him ...

Honestly, he never got any messages from her lips. Every time his gaze fell to her perfect mouth, his desire stole all good intentions away. In the last century, they never once got carried away.

His gaze dipped lower to allow him to refocus. Gwin knit his skin slowly. The pulse of energy from her hands fueled him until the next time he could afford this nearness.

Lance was in love with Gwin. His love was pure, chaste. The definition of chivalry. He would never hold her close. He would never taste her lips. He would never soothe the ache of his body with hers. That was not how their story would end.

Lance knew Gwin did not love Merlin. He'd known it the moment he'd seen the two together. There was no passion in her gaze, only duty. Their marriage had been a business transaction, like so many during that time period in which they were all born. Love was a luxury that most couldn't afford. The union between Gwin Galahad and Merlin Pendragon was an effort to seal a power alliance, and it did the trick, sacrificing three hearts in the process.

No. Two hearts. Lance didn't believe the eldest Pendragon had such an organ. The man couldn't lift a finger to protect his wife. Merlin had never gazed on Gwin with love, only with greed for her healing powers.

It was Lance who protected her. Lance who would slay dragons for her. Lance who would bleed for her.

She was an unattainable queen married to a wicked king. She was the untouchable Virgin Mary he devoutly worshiped. She was a dream he could never possess.

He knew he wasn't worthy of a physical love between them. Not with his base origins into this physical world. Lance loved Gwin on a higher level. A level that did not require the physical.

It was enough to know that she felt the same. It was the fact that she held him in such high regard that she would never think to ask him to break their vows. That pure devotion made him love her even more. Gwin had always looked at him, spoken to him, and treated him as the noblest of men. He would do nothing to cast shade on that great opinion of himself.

"There," she said. "You're healed."

Lance looked down at his arm. Damn. He'd thought that cut was a bit deeper. Fool fencing blade.

"You promise to be more careful on your next quest?"

It's what she always said to him after she healed his wounds. Lance never made such a promise to her. He would never lie to her.

"The town rests easy knowing you are on guard, Sir Lancelot."

"The town has my heart and my sword, milady."

"The town would be lost without you. You mean so much to us." She still had her hand on his bicep.

The energy pulsing between them was magic, but of a different kind. It would take nothing for him to lean in and capture her lips. It would cost him everything to do it.

He'd break his vow. He'd ruin his reputation. Even worse, he'd drag this noble lady down with him.

Still, neither could he lean entirely away from her. His entire being was entrenched in her.

Lance took a deep breath, making sure to take in a healthy dose of her floral scent. Then he took the first step in the process of moving away from her. It was an arduous, tiring task. But it was necessary. The two of them knew what was between them. Still, they had to keep up appearances with the rest of the town.

Gwin's fingers slowly, reluctantly released their hold on Lance's arm. As her thumb took lift off, the door to the Throne Room was thrown wide open. A beautiful blonde woman darkened the doorway.

"Mother?" Gwin yanked her fingers from Lance as though his rough skin burned her delicate hands.

Lady Galahad's shrewd gaze took in the ornate furnishings, the majestic Round Table. She squinted her eyes as though she found the decor wanting. Then she zeroed in on her daughter.

Gwin's proud shoulders hunched under her mother's assault. Her chin dipped. Her hands pressed together, her fingers wringing as they folded into her palms.

"I arrived twenty minutes ago," said Gwynfhar. "The Lady of the Castle wasn't there to greet me."

"I'm sorry," said Gwin. "I had other duties to tend to."

"*Other* duties." Gwynfhar didn't give Lance her notice. She didn't have to. Her tone spoke volumes. "Your husband needs you."

Gwin's shoulders dropped in earnest now. Her eyes rolled, and her words came out on a weary sigh. "What is the matter now?"

"I'm sure I don't know." Gwynfhar's tone was clipped and precise. Her words finely honed weapons whose sharp points she aimed at her daughter. "I'm not the man's wife."

Gwin's throat worked as though she had trouble swallowing her mother's words. After a moment, she lifted her chin, straightened her shoulders, and walked toward the door. But not before giving Lance an apologetic glance over her shoulder.

Lance lifted the corner of his mouth to tell her that he was okay. With that assurance, Gwin continued out of the Throne Room. Unfortunately, her mother remained.

Lance was not surprised when the older woman didn't follow her daughter out. Lance's father hadn't been the only one vocal about his shortcomings when it came to Gwin. His father passed shortly after the sword abandoned him.

Gwynfhar stood silent and stoic in the doorway. Lance tried to pretend that her silence didn't bother him. That lasted all of five seconds.

"I was wounded." Lance waved at the healed skin.

"What's broken inside of you, my daughter cannot heal."

And with that final warning shot, Gwynfhar left the room. She didn't look back. She didn't need to see that her aim had been perfect. She'd hit her target dead on in the vulnerable part of him that was Lance's sense of worth.

Even after all these years, after all his great deeds, after he bled for this town, still he wasn't good enough.

4

———

*N*ight had fallen in the town of Camelot. Gwin walked past a window and saw the dotting lights of fireflies. Their sparkling tails were clear to see in the dimming light of the day. The creatures loved the long grasses of the moat surrounding the castle.

She remembered catching the illuminating bugs as a child. They'd flown over her head. Their wings beating to move their small bodies just beyond her reach.

Gwin couldn't use magic to catch them. They'd hide from any light but their own. So witch fire drove them away. The little witch and wizard children had to catch them the human way.

It had taken her hours but Gwin had managed to

catch a jarful and bring them inside. Her mother had shrieked in abject horror and disgust and made her throw them out.

She'd never touched one again. But she remained fascinated by their light. Even now, as a woman grown, they flew above her head. Their light sparkling even as the last few shards of daylight dimmed as they flew about freely.

"What did I tell you about being near that boy," said Gwynfhar.

"He's not a boy, mother. He's a knight. The best knight in all of Camelot."

"He's a bastard."

Lance stepped out of the Throne Room. Just in time to hear the insult. He lifted his head high and walked proudly down the hall.

Gwin tried to catch his eye, to communicate her apology for her mother's words. She and Lance never needed words between them. He knew that wasn't how she felt about him. But a man's pride was a fragile thing. And so, he wouldn't look at her.

They'd been so close just a few moments ago. His gaze had shone down on her, making her twinkle under its brilliance. She'd felt like she could fly. She'd felt so full of light that it burst out of her.

Until her mother shrieked in horror and sent him away.

As a child, Gwin had let the fireflies go without much argument. She knew she could only hold them captive for a day before they'd die. Her time with Lance was always stolen moments before she had to release him back into the world.

She was tired of letting him slip away from her. She wanted to hold him captive forever. She wanted to argue for him to stay. She wanted to wrap her legs around him like she'd seen a woman do in the movies.

But that would never work. Gwin never wore pants. She'd have to lift her skirts to perform such a feat.

She shook the damnable thought from her head. She could never do such a thing. She was bound to another. She had made her choice. And she had to live with it. Trapped in a jar of her own making, even as it crushed the light from her soul and the soul of the man she loved.

Back when she was a child, she'd seen a man crush the bugs in their hands. All to see their hands glow with stolen light. That had been Merlin.

It should've been a foreshadow of events to come.

"You are a married woman." Her mother hissed once Lance turned the corner and melted into others from the community. "You should be with your husband."

"You mean the murderous wizard who killed witches and nearly ended your youngest daughter?"

This wasn't the first time Merlin had been at death's door. He'd gone missing two decades ago. Everyone had thought him dead. But when witches across the ley line grid that spanned the earth began turning up with their magic drained, Gwin immediately suspected her dearly departed husband hadn't entirely departed the living world.

Siphoning magic was a trick he'd learned from her. She would take the crippling power that wracked his body and replace it with her gentle, healing magic. Merlin wasn't so gentle when he practiced the maneuver on others. He took everything, crushing the witches' spirits until his hands glowed with their stolen essence.

He was even at fault for taking Morgan's magic. But Gwin's baby sister was a force to be reckoned with. After he'd knocked her down, Morgan had managed to get back on her feet with her power in tow.

Yet, Merlin still had Gwin under his thumb. Even

now she could feel his greedy hands reaching out, trying to wrap around her person and crush her light.

No. Wait. That was her mother.

Gwin inhaled under the weight of her mother's glare. She lifted her chin, but the weight of the world was on her shoulders, leaving her feeling lightheaded.

"You were called to a higher purpose." Her mother began the speech that always turned Gwin's mind. Gwin often wondered if it were a spell. "With your gifts, it is your responsibility to do your duty. These people need your guidance."

"Morgan is marrying Arthur, the heir. She will take over as Lady of the Castle. It's her they should look to."

"Your sister doesn't have your skill, your strength. She knows it, as does everyone in this town."

"Morgan is stronger than you think."

"She's in love," her mother scoffed. "Love of a man isn't higher than love of duty."

Gwin looked away. The words were working.

"Your husband needs you. What will you do when he dies? Who will you be?"

That was the point. Gwin could be anything she wanted when Merlin died. Maybe she could even finally kiss the ginger knight she had dreamed of every night for over a hundred years.

"You gave Camelot no child."

That was a sore spot. Weight crashed down on Gwin in shame. The shame was heavy.

"Perhaps it's not too late," said her mother. "Your husband still has life in his blood and seed in his loins."

Gwin reared back. Gwynfhar and her daughters didn't have a close mother-daughter relationship. Gwin knew her mother was an opportunist and a social climber. But she never dreamed she'd steer her daughter in such a direction.

"You go too far." Gwin jerked away from her mother and stormed down the hall. Unfortunately, the direction she was headed was just as distasteful. She was headed to the infirmary to check on her villainous husband.

5

———

*L*ance balled and unballed his fists. After all these years, Lady Gwynfhar still got to him.

It was likely because she had the face of the woman he loved stretched across her disapproving features.

The thought of Gwin's rejection was his worst nightmare. So whenever he encountered his true love's mother and her pinched face, his every doubt, his every misgiving, his every shame rose to the surface. It was cruel.

He didn't expect Gwin to stand up for him in the face of her mother. There wasn't much she could say if she did. Lance's own mother had been a fallen woman. She'd fallen in love. She hadn't known it was with someone else's husband. When she found out, her heart fell in its cage. It broke and never got up again.

But she never fell into a life where she sold her body. She worked in factories, anything to keep a roof over her boy's head and food in his belly. Her life was hard and came to an abrupt ending. As she lay dying, she told Lance the truth of his heritage.

Lance made his way from the remote Cairngorm Mountains of Scotland, where his father thought no one would know about his bastard, to Wales where the magical town of Camelot rested. He found his father sitting in the lap of luxury on a high seat of nobility. The welcome was anything but welcoming. But Lance's parentage was undeniable.

His father wanted no part of him. Neither did his stepmother. Only the sword, the knights, and Gwin had.

The townsfolk weren't sure how to treat the illegitimate son of a revered knight. There were those that shrugged off his father's transgressions. There were others who were scandalized. They looked upon Lance as though his conception and existence were his faults.

It had never mattered to Gwin. She didn't see the bad in anybody. Including her mother and her husband. Add that to the thousands of reasons Lance loved her.

Gwin had never once said a harsh word to him. Or looked at him as though he didn't belong. She'd raised a hand to him once—the day they formally met. But that had been his fault. It was also a memory he cherished.

And with that memory, he was smiling again. His consciousness of Gwynfhar's frown was a distant thought as he turned down a deserted hall. He looked up to find he wasn't alone.

"Good eve, good sir."

Lance tried not to outwardly sigh at Lady Minerva's sudden appearance. She was a woman in the prime of life and still lovely. Her husband, on the other hand, was wheelchair-bound after valiantly defending Camelot for decades. For his troubles, he was saddled with her.

"I'm so glad you're here, good sir." Lady Minerva's breaths came in little pants. "I'm having trouble with my corset."

She tugged, but her fingers couldn't reach the silky ribbon of the stays at her back. She looked distressed, but Lance didn't budge.

"What appears to be the problem, my lady?"

"The problem is the corset is still on." Her stiff

fingers became nimble, and she grasped the length of ribbon. Her stays unraveled, her corset loosened, her bosom spilled out and she launched herself into his chest.

Lance deftly moved aside, making room for her to fling herself into the wall behind him. But, because he wasn't a bastard, he reached out and steadied her before she crashed and fell on her ass.

"I'm sure you'll find a lady nearby to help you," said Lance. "Or you can go and seek out the assistance of your husband."

With that, Lance gave the curtest of bows and turned on his heel. Because manners precluded him from turning his back on a lady, he held there as she continued her unwanted seduction.

"Why must you continue to play these games, Lancelot? You've been stuck in town for far too long with nothing but untouchable witches and no human women to dally with and assuage your baser urges. You must be starved for attention."

Lance had no base urges. He'd spent his entire life fighting for respectability and protecting his honor. Yet every so often, more often than not, a bored lady or a randy widow would approach him in an effort to debase him. As though his valor, all the glory he'd won for this town, mattered less than the itch in their corsets.

"I can ease your troubles. No one needs to know."

So that he could be another high-born's dirty little secret, just like his father had done to his mother. The hair at the nape of Lance's neck stiffened.

"I'm trouble free, thank you, my lady." Lance turned on his heel giving Lady Minerva his back. There was no courteous bow this time.

"I know you poked Lady Prudence with your broadsword last year."

Lady Prudence was another bored, old witch who liked to accost Lance in the halls of Camelot. She'd even made her way into his bedroom once. That's when he, the most valiant knight at the Round Table, in the safest place in the whole world, began locking and barring his door at night.

Lady Minerva wasn't done. She rounded him, her hand on her bodice to keep from spilling any further. "I ruined my life when I chose him. If only you had come along earlier. We could've been together. We could be together now. My husband is dying. I want to be with you; a strong, virile, young man before my life is over. I don't want to wait any longer for my life to begin."

Lance couldn't hide the disgust from his face any longer. He made a choking sound. Lady Minerva's features turned from pleading to pissed.

"You think you're high and mighty because you're a knight. But we all know the truth. Beneath your virtuous and chivalrous facade, you're still the son of a whore."

Lance fought to keep his feet moving. There were people rounding the corner. If she continued her foul diatribe, they all would hear. So, he tried to let it go. And failed.

Attacks on his honor were one thing, he was used to it. But attacks on his mother he did not countenance. He turned and stormed up to Lady Minerva.

She backtracked, her back slamming into the wall in her haste. But she did it with a smile on her face. He'd heard that she liked it rough. So rough she'd get.

"Trouble with your corset, you said?" He reached out. He gripped the bottom of her stays and pulled.

"Yes, my lord." She breathed, eyes closed in ecstasy. She reached up to wrap her hands around his neck. But he ducked away from her snare.

"I'll take these to Igraine for you."

Lady Minerva's eyes slammed open. Igraine was an empath. She could see the past and future by simply touching a person's belongings.

"You wouldn't dare," she hissed.

"I consider it my duty and my honor."

Lance turned and stormed away, tossing the ribbon aside as he did. Lady Minerva didn't follow. Her clothing was coming apart. But that was her problem.

He made his way down to the dungeons, still irate from his encounter with Lady Gwynfhar and now Lady Minerva. No matter his great deeds, nor his careful protection of his reputation, he still couldn't escape the mark drawn on him by his father's misdeeds.

He descended down into the bowels of the castle. Warmth did not reach this deep. Cold seeped from the stones into his boots.

Entering the dungeons, Lance found Percy and Arthur already in progress of the interrogation of Simon Accolon, Malegant's son. The man of science was barefoot. His once crisp, white, collared shirt was now dingy and sweat dampened. His air of academic superiority was replaced with a caged desperation as he stood behind bars.

"I don't know what else you want me to say," came Accolon's voice. "My father was crazy. My mother didn't allow too many visitations with him when I was growing up. He was always going on about Friday the 13th. When I was a kid, I thought he was talking about the movie. I didn't understand the significance of that day and the Templars."

A kid growing up in the modern human world would naturally assume the reference was made to the movie. Few understood the true significance of that date in history and the Templars.

The history of The Poor Fellow-Soldiers of Christ and of the Temple of Solomon began in France centuries ago. Their original mission had been to grant safe passage to witches and wizards back to the Holy Lands from which their ancestors came. For two hundred years they carried out this mission, later including the devout in their safe passage. But as the Templars' ranks grew, so did the jealousy of the crown and the church.

It all came to a head in France when King Phillip and Pope Clement conspired to rid themselves of the Templars and relieve the order of the riches they'd amassed. In a coordinated effort, they gathered up thousands of knights on a single day. Many were arrested and jailed, even more died. This all happened on Friday the 13th, 1306.

The day the order, as the world knew it, died. What rose from the ashes was the antithesis of what the original Templars had been. Now under the control of the crown and the cross, they hunted down anything magical and destroyed it.

"You know, it's kind of stuffy down here." Accolon tugged at his drooping collar. "My allergies have been acting up. Do you think I could get out for some fresh air?"

The knights all glared at the man, especially Arthur. Apparently, Accolon didn't understand that the only thing keeping him alive was the bars that separated him from Arthur. That, and any knowledge he could give them about his father's whereabouts and plan.

"My father would go on and on about the lost army of the Templars," said Accolon.

"They're not lost," said Percy. "They're dead."

Accolon shrugged. "After what I've seen this past year, I'm not so sure anymore."

Humans' eyes had been opened to flying dragons, angels coming up from the core of the earth, and God delivering a sermon from the sky. Most chose to believe what the government said, that it was all a hoax. But there were a few believers of the truth; God and Her angels, the Elohim, lived in the core of the Earth with many extinct animals. The core was only one of the many realms on this planet that humans knew nothing about.

Accolon let out a fit of coughing before he continued. "My father said there was a sleeping army of the devout. He seemed to believe they were under a spell."

"An army of the devout?" asked Lance.

"Thousands of Templars died during the Friday Massacre," said Accolon. "But not all the bodies were found. Hundreds were unaccounted for."

"Malegant thinks they're sleeping somewhere?" said Arthur. "For hundreds of years."

"You're looking pretty good for two centuries."

Arthur growled low in his throat.

Accolon backed up, hands raised. "That was a c-c-" He sneezed and began another coughing fit.

"That's all I know," said Accolon after the fit of coughing. He really wasn't looking so good. "He believed magic would break the curse of their sleep."

"Magic can't bring people back from the dead," said Lance.

Though as he said it he looked at Arthur. Accolon had shot Arthur straight in the heart with a gun. Morgan had used magic to bring Arthur back. But Lance was sure that incident didn't count because Arthur hadn't truly died. He'd just been wounded. Mortally. Or near mortally.

"This is a dead end," said Arthur. He looked at Accolon in disgust as the man continued his coughing fit.

"What about the note about Champagne and Hugo de Payens?" Lance asked Percy.

"De Payens betrayed Camelot," said Percy.

"But he also began the Templars," said Arthur. "And most of our records of the original Templar Order are still at the manse in Champagne. I should probably go check the libraries there, to see if there's any lead to what Malegant may be looking for."

The younger Malegant was coughing so rapidly, he was turning blue in the face. The knights leaned against the bars, watching the color change. Lance believed they dusted down here at least once a decade or so.

"You can't leave now," said Lance. "You're in the midst of wedding planning."

Arthur nodded his head as though to indicate that's why it was the perfect time to leave.

"Well, I can't miss another day," said Percy. "With

Geraint and Gawain still away, I'm in charge of squire training."

"I'll go," said Lance. "It's just a recon mission. I can do it alone."

Accolon had collapsed in a heap on the stone floor. No one moved as they looked down at the man. His chest still rose, but at least he'd stopped coughing and hacking. Lance knew Arthur wouldn't offer. He doubted Percy even thought about it.

"Fine," said Lance. "I'll take him up to the infirmary."

6

____

The farther Gwin got from the Throne Room and her mother, the freer she felt. All her life she'd done what her mother had asked of her, tried to live up to the image her mother saw of her. If she were honest, it left her nothing but misery.

She pulled on a fake smile every day of her life. She pulled it on to be accepted by those in the town. She pulled it on to be welcoming to those visiting. She plastered it on to marry a man she did not love.

Every day her face strained from holding up the smile of complacency. And now she was tired.

She'd thought her life would be in service as Lady of the Castle. But, now that her husband was dying, and her sister was marrying the remaining

Pendragon heir, and her services were no longer needed, Gwin's veneer began to crack.

It didn't matter what Morgan said about not wanting the role of Lady of the Castle. With no husband and no heir, the title wasn't rightfully Gwin's any longer. In truth, it had never truly been hers.

But she'd done her duty as best she could. Now she would be relieved. And relief assailed her.

For the first time, she wondered what it would be like if she had chosen a different life. What would it be like if she didn't tend to the needs of others? What if she only thought of herself?

Morgan had placed herself first all her life. Her sister was carefree and happy and now she'd found the love of her life. Loren did the same. She put her needs first and went on adventures. She was never want for male attention and company. Neither of them ever wore a fake smile or shouldered more weight than they could bear.

What would that be like?

Gwin could run barefoot through the castle halls and out to the grounds. She could leave the ledgers until it was time to pay taxes. She could have ice cream for breakfast and pancakes for dinner.

She could step into the embrace of a certain

knight. She could do it when he had no wound. She'd finally be allowed to tend to his heart. She wouldn't have to hold back when her lips ached to kiss his. She would lean in and claim him.

The sound of coughing broke her dream. Gwin looked up to see that her feet had taken her straight to the infirmary. Inside the open door she spied her husband. Merlin wheezed and hacked as though he were on his deathbed. Because he was on his deathbed.

Gwin stared at her husband from the doorway. Had she ever loved him? No. She had not. Had she ever cared? Yes, she had.

Merlin's frail body shook hard with the next batch of coughs. Just like it had when he was a young man. When she had first met Merlin, Gwin had been sitting near him in the Great Hall. She'd watched his mother tend to him, concern etched on Lady Merylin's pretty face.

Something had pulled young Gwin, just at the tender age of ten, to the two of them. Perhaps it was the magic inside her wanting to help? Perhaps it was the unconditional love on Lady Merylin's face?

Gwin had made her way over to the pair. She'd placed her hand on Merlin's heart. She'd pulled the illness out of him.

Merlin had looked down at her in wonder. Lady Merylin had too. She'd gathered Gwin to herself and hugged her. The embrace had at first startled, and then delighted, Gwin. Her mother wasn't the affectionate type. There were only nods of acknowledgment. Never embraces.

Merlin's illness was soul deep. The healing magic had been a temporary fix. One that she would repeat a countless number of times in the next fifty years of their life together; siphoning off energy from him. It was her special talent; releasing the burdens of others.

Now, on the metal frame bed of the infirmary, Merlin's body shook once more. She'd never seen him get this bad. What if this was it? What if this was his end? What if he were about to die?

Gwin moved to take a step into the room, but her foot wouldn't settle over the threshold.

If she went into that room and saved him, it would be another day, another week, another month with the burden of him. If he slipped away she could be at peace, she could have a new life. The life she'd only ever dreamed about.

No one would miss him. He'd murdered witches to stay alive. Yet here she stood preparing to drain herself to save him again.

His eyes found hers. A cruel smile slivered across his pale, thin, cracked lips. "So, you're finally going to do it. You're finally going to let me die."

Merlin chuckled but it was an awful, creaking, wheezing sound.

"Then you and your lover can come out of the shadows and dance on my grave."

Gwin stormed into the room. "Lance and I have never-"

But her words were lost as Merlin hacked and coughed. Gwin balled her fists. The magic in her ached to reach out and correct what was wrong with a suffering soul.

They had been friends once. Hadn't they? She was no longer certain.

Had they always been more nurse and patient? Lady Merylin was the only one who had asked Gwin if she was certain of the pairing. Whatever answer Gwin gave satisfied the mother. It was that satisfaction that Gwin held onto through the first months of her marriage as Merlin's cruelty surfaced.

Gwin had thought she wore a facade. It had nothing on the facade her husband cloaked himself in. Merlin's mask had even fooled his own mother.

Still, Gwin thought the light within her would win. That it would heal the wounded beast that showed its dark colors. She'd been wrong. Merlin had crushed her like a firefly only to watch the light die out in his palm.

"Heal me, damn you," he said now. "It is your duty as my wife."

For the first time in her life, Gwin's palms cooled. Her skin itched to maim instead of burned to aide. "You were never a true husband to me. Not in any sense of the word."

"Careful how loudly you say those words. You don't want them to know, do you?"

Gwin hugged her arms to herself, empty hands spanning her forearms. It was the only time she was hugged outside of the children in the town. Once Lady Merylin passed away, her husband never once offered an ounce of affection.

"You don't want them to know you've been living a lie all this time. That you're not really what you say you are. You are not the Lady of the Castle."

"And whose fault is that?" She wrenched her arms from herself, unleashing a deep well of anger and sorrow. "I offered you all of myself."

"More lies. You kept your heart away."

"You didn't want my heart," she said. "All you ever wanted was my magic."

"All you ever wanted was my title. We both got what we wanted out of this sham of a union."

"I wanted to love you. I tried. I wanted children. But you—"

Merlin's eyes cut to her, and Gwin jerked back. He was helpless on the bed, but he still had the power to make her cower.

"Be grateful for what you have now," he said. "Once I die, it will all be taken from you. You will no longer have your title. If you're not careful, I'll take your respect away too when I die. I'll let the whole town know that you've been perpetrating a lie for a century. I'll let them know this marriage was never consummated, that there is no bond."

It was true. Gwin had come to Merlin on their wedding night ready to perform her duty as a wife. But he'd been sick. So it continued on for months. Until finally she learned the truth. Merlin could not perform as a husband would with his wife.

She kept his secret. Like she kept all his secrets. Now she stood in the artificial light of the sick room. Her light dimming as his mere presence continued to crush her spirit.

Merlin had stopped coughing. He was gasping for breath now. His face turning pale and now blue.

Nausea rolled through her body as she watched

him convulse. She couldn't take watching another creature suffer. She had to do something.

But if she let this happen, if she let his illness consume him, it would end all *her* suffering. And maybe his as well.

But no. Not like this. She couldn't countenance this type of pain on even her worst enemy, and her husband was the villain of her life.

And so Gwin reached for him. Merlin's eyes bulged out of his head with his next cough. Even though her hands were on him, he felt beyond her reach. The pain was too intense, even for her. It rattled her as she dug deep inside herself to give him what he needed to live.

"Not like this," she cried. "I'm sorry. Come back. I'll fix it. Come back."

Merlin gasped in a breath. His eyes opened and he looked at her with hatred and accusation. Then his eyes rolled back in his head. He'd passed out, but he was alive.

Gwin sighed. In relief? In defeat?

She lifted her head to find Lance standing in the door.

7

———

Lance walked into the infirmary on stiff and weary legs. He carried a heavy load on his back. He set Simon Accolon down on one of the beds. The man jostled. Accolon had been out of it as Lance had carried him up the stairs. But now the scientist's curious eyes were open and rapt on Gwin.

Lance, himself, was still dazed at the sight he'd walked in on. Merlin had been on his deathbed for months now. The only thing keeping him in this world was Gwin.

As Lance had come into the infirmary, it looked as though the sycophant was making his final exit. That was until Gwin yanked him back on the stage.

With his back released from the heavy burden,

Lance's shoulders drooped. A numbness settled over his shoulder blades. It was her right to save him. Her duty as a healer... and as his wife. She had the power to give him new life.

Still, Lance died a little every time she reached out to save the miserable man's life.

Gwin lifted her gifted hands and made her way to Lance. She moved hesitantly. Like she was a doe approaching danger.

Didn't she know he would never do anything to harm her? His feelings wouldn't allow it. Beyond his vows, his heart, his mind, his body was hers to command. He'd fall on his sword if she asked him. It would likely hurt less than the agony he felt in this moment.

His heart yearned to reach out to her as she came near. He ached to pull her into his arms and offer her more than his sword for safety. He wanted to offer her his body for comfort. His soul for refuge.

He looked away, as he often had to when they weren't alone. At the moment, every feeling was clear on his face. If she looked into his eyes, she'd see. She'd see all of his desires and his pain. She didn't need that burden on top of all her others. He fastened his gaze to the floor.

"Lance—" she began but was cut off.

"How did you do that?" Accolon asked through his wheezing. "How did you heal that man? Is it a direct energy transfer?"

Both Gwin and Lance focused on the inquisitive human sitting erect on the infirmary bed across from Merlin's. It was safer to give Accolon his attention than for Lance to address Gwin directly.

"He's having some sort of allergic reaction," Lance said.

"Are you able to create the energy within yourself?" Accolon continued. "Does your skin open when the elemental substance comes out of you?"

Gwin walked calmly over to Accolon. She placed her hand on the man's shoulder. Instantly, he stopped talking. Lance felt the pulse of magic extend through her fingertips. There was a quiet thud. Accolon's eyes closed, and he slumped down into slumber.

Merlin slept peacefully too. Alive and peaceful after Gwin's desperate plea and hasty treatment.

"Lance, I—"

"I'll leave you to your duties, my lady."

Lance turned on his heel but he couldn't move. Gwin had grabbed his bicep. The wound from earlier had long since healed. There was no reason for her to touch him, except that she wanted him to stay and hear her.

He could've easily broken her hold. But she held too much power over him. Besides, a chivalrous man never gave his back to a lady.

He turned back around. But he kept his gaze on the floor.

"I almost let him die."

Her voice was shaky. The desperation of her tone had him looking up. Gone was the vibrant creature of his waking dreams. What was left was a shell, a frail woman. Lance did not like it one bit.

"I was going to let him go," she said, looking down at her hands. "He's caused so much pain."

"That's not who you are," he said.

"No," she agreed, meeting his gaze. "It's not who I am. This isn't who I want to be."

Gwin stepped closer to him. Her gaze dipped to his chest. Her hands came up to his heart, but they did not land yet. Lance's heart pounded hard against its cage to get at its master.

And then, with the lightest of touches, Gwin's gentle fingertips crashed into him. Her feather-light touch nearly knocked him over. But that wasn't the end of it.

Lance could only watch the descent of her head.

It was like an earthquake when her blonde head landed at the center of his chest. It knocked his world off kilter.

She looked so exhausted, so in need. Lance didn't hesitate. His arms were around her in the next instant. Gwin sighed into him, and he knew heaven.

He'd been this close to her before. The first time they'd met. They'd had a few occasions to dance at balls in the Great Halls and festivals in front of the whole town. She'd come close to harm's way once or twice, and he'd used his body to shield hers.

But this was different. Now she sought comfort, not entertainment or protection.

"I ruined my life when I chose him," she said. "If only you had come along earlier. We could've been together."

Was this real life? Had he fallen asleep while walking into the infirmary? He was living his fantasy. Or perhaps he was under a cruel spell now?

These were the words he'd dreamed of hearing for decades. But now they sailed to his ears from her lips. Not from his heart to his deepest desires.

"We could be together now." Gwin lifted her head and gazed up at him.

Like always, Lance became lost in those blue eyes. He always had trouble sailing because the sea reminded him of her eyes. He'd become lost in the churning of the waves.

"My husband is dying."

Lance nodded at that fact. He felt no shame for his joy in it. Merlin was a scourge. Lance had seen it the first moment he'd met the man. He knew it for certain as he'd watched Gwin over the years pulling on a brave front while shackled to a monster.

"I want to be with you." The words left her lips, but reached him over a vast and tormented sea.

Even in his wildest dreams, he'd never taken things this far. But Gwin was not done living out his fantasy. Her hands were moving. They left his heart and were climbing his chest, up over his shoulders.

"I don't want to wait any longer for my life to begin."

Her fingers brushed the hairs at the nape of his neck, and his knees buckled. She gave a tug of his head, and he obeyed. Lance bent his head down to her, to hear whatever her lips wanted to tell him. What her lips had to say was in a kiss.

The scent of flowers distracted him. He'd some-times walk the halls of Camelot at night, taking the paths she frequented. He did this searching out a hint of that delicate scent that was hers alone. When he found a trace, he'd fill his nose. The scent always went straight to his head and clouded his judgment.

If this were a battle, he'd have been outmatched before he'd ever drawn his weapon. Her lower lip struck him first, brushing softly against his upper lip. Some small voice inside of him told him to retreat, that this was a losing battle, and the scars that resulted would never heal.

The voice went mute when Gwin lunged past the millimeter of space between them and closed the distance. Her slender arms came up behind his head and struck down around his neck. Lance's hands rose to parry the attack, capturing her slender waist and pulling her flush against his body.

They held like that for seconds, for moments, for the century they'd been denied this closeness. The kiss remained a light brushing of lips. Her lips caught his upper lip in a pliable hold. His lower lip cradled hers in a supple grip.

And they held. Barely breathing. Not moving. As though they both were afraid that any minute shift would break the moment and rob them of this small slice of pure, unadulterated bliss.

"Gwin, we're about to head out to look at linens for the reception. You have to come and save me from mother—Oh!"

Gwin jerked away from him. But Lance, who had excellent reflexes, was slow to react. His hands didn't release her. His lips still buzzed from the kiss. His gaze was hazy as he reluctantly moved from the dream world back to reality. When he opened his eyes the younger Galahad sister came into focus.

Morgan's blue gaze was a few shades darker than Gwin's. Now her eyes were bright with shock. Then her lips split into a grin. "Do not let me interrupt."

Morgan stepped forward and held up her hand in a fist to dap her sister. But Gwin turned away, her face flushed. Undaunted, Morgan winked at Lance. Then she turned and walked out of the infirmary pulling the door shut.

The door snicked closed. Lance stared at the closed door that concealed them. He jumped when Gwin reached out to him. Her cheeks were flushed with red. Not the pink of embarrassment. The shade was the color of shame.

"It was only Morgan," she said. "No one else saw."

Lance stepped back. Her words were an unexpected punch to his gut, followed by a stunning slice to his heart.

"Lance?" Gwin stepped to him. Her hands were raised, aimed for his heart. Her eyes were imploring, pleading her case to his soul. Perfect, proper, poised Lady Gwin fumbled over her words as she spoke. "I want to be with you."

"I have to go." He spoke the words as though he were a disembodied spirit. He did not feel in control of his body, or his emotions, or his thoughts. Nothing made sense.

Gwin's shoulders slumped forward as though his words hit her hard. Her face fell. The redness returned. It was a lighter shade this time. A delicate pink whose hue spoke of self-consciousness and not guilt.

The weight settled on her shoulders and she hunched. But he couldn't lift this burden. Not with her. Never with her.

His love for her was pure. She was the best thing in his life. The reason he knew he was good.

And she'd kissed him.

She'd kissed him while her husband lay dying in the bed behind them. She'd kissed him in secret behind a closed door. She'd kissed him and didn't want anyone else to know.

Lance walked away from her, pulling the door open, and shutting it and her behind him.

8

———

Gwin had just kissed Lance.

She'd dreamed of it for years. Not during the day while the sun shone and everyone saw her face. But every night as darkness fell, the dreams came to her.

They were pretty PG dreams. She knew what happened between a man and a woman in the bedroom, of course. She was a witch, after all. Witches were taught from a young age that their bodies were temples and worthy of praise and adoration and pleasure.

However, learning about a process and experiencing the process were two entirely different things. She'd read about the press of lips to another's, but the feeling in real life was unexpected. Lance's mouth had been pillow soft and warm. At the same time, his lips had been firm and unyielding. The two polarities fascinated her as they wouldn't fit in neat compartments in her brain.

She'd fit snug in the cage of his arms. She'd found a quiet peace in the pounding of his chest.

The few kisses she'd shared with Merlin paled in bleak comparison. Lance's single kiss was a firework display worthy of a celebration of national independence. He tasted spicy. The taste of him was still on the tip of her tongue. Everything in her throbbed. She ached for relief.

It had been magic. It had been divine. It had been her dream come true. It was her new truth.

Lance had kissed her like he'd been drowning and she was his first taste of air. But now she was alone again, and she couldn't understand why.

Had she done something wrong? Had her inexperience turned him off? Had her lack of skill turned him away?

Before he'd left, his gaze had shuttered, closing her out. He'd never done that with her. He'd always let her see into the heart of him. What didn't he want her to see now?

Perhaps there was someone else?

Of course, there was someone else. Gwin had

chosen to marry another. She never expected Lance to spend his nights alone. She didn't expect it, and she didn't like to think of it.

Lance had always kept any evidence of a lover hidden from her view. She had heard stories. But she never believed most of them. Lance would never tarry with a widow of the town or dally with a married witch. It was so far beneath his character that it was laughable.

Gwin balled her hands into fists to know that anyone could even think such behaviors of him. As she clenched her fist, the ring on her finger burned her palm as her indignation flared.

Gwin looked down at it. Then over at her sleeping husband. Her heart pounded in her ears. Her lips burned with a different heat as she ran the events of a few moments ago back through her mind. She, a married woman, had thrown herself on him, the most devout knight of his time.

But this was different. They were different.

Surely Lance couldn't think that of her. Could he? He knew how she felt about him. Didn't he? He of all people had to know who her heart truly beat for. Hadn't he?

"Oh, Gwin, I am so sorry."

Gwin pulled herself out of her reverie to find

Morgan had returned to the infirmary. Her sister was beaming at her, bouncing on her toes as she walked toward her.

"I'm so sorry," Morgan repeated. "I did not mean to interrupt and scare him away."

Gwin turned her sister's words over in her head. Lance had held her close until Morgan interrupted them. In fact, it had been Gwin who'd pulled away from him.

They both knew that if they had been caught in an embrace it would be the end of their reputations, and their reputations mattered a great deal to both of them. He had to know Morgan wouldn't tell anybody, not until they were ready.

Gwin was done hiding her desires, done putting others before her. She'd make sure Lance knew that. As soon as she found him.

"Are you okay?" Morgan asked.

"I am."

She was. And now that her mind had worked out the logical answer to the problem, all of the feelings rushed back in. A flood of emotion rose to her cheeks and spread across her shoulders. Her lips tingled from the memory of being pressed against him.

"I just kissed Lance."

"Yeah, you did." Morgan's grin was wide and proud of her older sister's carnal activity.

Gwin's face flushed, but it was a flush of joy. Happiness hit her so hard she had to reach out for the wall to steady herself.

A rustle had her turning her head. Merlin shifted in the bed. He didn't open his eyes, but his breathing became raspy and labored. Gwin's smile faltered.

"No. Uhn-uhn," Morgan said. "Do not go there."

To further emphasize her point, Morgan rounded on Gwin so that she blocked her view of Merlin.

"He never loved you," Morgan continued. She lifted her hand ticking off Merlin's transgressions against Gwin one by one. "He used you. He left you. He tried to kill you. He tried to kill your cousin. He nearly killed me. I, for one, am done tiptoeing around the issue. If he doesn't hurry up and die soon, you're getting a divorce."

It was interesting. Not too long ago, the D word would've sent Gwin into an apoplectic fit. Now, the D word didn't scare her so much. In fact, the thought of that word sent a sense of relief through her.

"You deserve to be happy," said Morgan.

"Yeah. I do," Gwin said. "I love him."

"I have to assume we're talking about Lance."

"Yes."

"Well, duh. The whole town knows the two of you love each other."

Had they been so obvious all this time? And no one scolded them? Then no one would be shocked when they announced they were together.

"What are you waiting for?" Morgan grasped Gwin's forearms and squeezed. "Go find that man and jump his bones."

Gwin's blush deepened. She'd just had her first real kiss. Sex? With Lance? Was she ready for that? She was just getting used to the idea that she could kiss him. Maybe hold his hand in public. Announce their feelings to the world instead of trying, unsuccessfully, to hide them.

But she could have sex now. She could do anything now. First, she needed to find Lance.

9

---

*L*ance walked in a daze down the hall. His head did not mind where his feet led him.

Before he knew it, he was in the residential area of the castle.

He'd climbed three flights without noticing. What he did notice was whose door he stood before. In the century that he'd had occasion to live in this castle, never had he once dared to come down this path.

Even though he'd run from her, his body still led him back to her. He'd followed her scent like a hound in heat. Picking at the tendrils in the air, he'd come to stand at Gwin's bedroom door.

His heart pounded, pushing against his rib cage,

which pushed against the fabric of his shirt. His ears rang with the phantom sounds of her voice, her laugh. The way she'd sighed into his mouth.

For years, he'd taken in the scent of her through his nose. Now he knew what she tasted like. A nectar so sweet bees would cease their honey production in favor of her breath.

Lance leaned his head against Gwin's doorframe. He pressed his hands into the hard, cold wood that kept him out. Everything in him urged him to bust the barrier down, even though he knew she wasn't in there. But he couldn't go back to where she was. If he did, he would definitely kiss her again.

Oh, God. He had kissed Gwin. His mind couldn't work out how it had happened?

She'd been sad, so sad. Near tears and weary. Of course, he'd been her strength when she was weakened. What kind of champion wouldn't have?

But then she'd looked up at him. The next thing he knew she was all around him, a part of him. Until she pulled away from him, shame and guilt replacing the sweet connection they'd shared.

Lance pushed away from her bedroom door. His steps unsteady as he puzzled out where to go. He couldn't go back to the infirmary. If he did, he'd have her in his arms again. And that would be a mistake.

Wouldn't it?

Yes. The answer was yes. That was why she'd pulled away from him when someone came into the door and seen them together. A kiss, an embrace, anything more, none of it could ever happen again. No matter how much his entire being craved it.

Lance slumped into a dark corner down a deserted hallway. For the first time in his life, he understood how a man could break his vows. Cheating was no longer a heinous idea. It was a logical possibility.

Hang his honor. Hang it right on her lower lip. He stood and began toward the infirmary again.

He couldn't remember why honor was so important to him. He would do anything to touch her again, everything be damned. She was within his grasp. Hell, he'd been in her grasp.

She'd been warm, soft curves. She'd been a sugar rush straight to the head. An ice cream that froze his brain. And like all things addictive, he wanted more. He couldn't just have one taste.

His steps stopped again before they hit the last rung on the stair that would bring him to the same level as the infirmary. What was he doing? He couldn't have another taste of Gwin. She was a married woman. That kiss couldn't have been her thinking. It had to have been his fault.

Somehow, some way, he had driven her to it. She was a noble lady. She would've never dreamed of lunging at him or pressing her lips to his.

But what of her words?

Gwin's words, so like Lady Minerva's, echoed at the back of Lance's mind.

I ruined my life when I chose him ...

If only you had come along earlier ...

I don't want to wait ...

Those words had Lance back-stepping down the stairs that would lead him out of the castle. He had not imagined that exchange. He had not made up the guilt and shame on Gwin's face when she thought they were caught. It all mirrored what he'd experienced earlier with Lady Minerva, with every woman who had propositioned him over the years thinking he'd break his vows for them.

Lance's world was crumbling around him, and so he did what he always did when the reality got too much for him. He ran into battle to prove his worth.

The door to the castle was in sight. He could cross the moat, grab a horse, and ride to run the energy out of him.

Before he could reach the door, a lady came into

his view. Lady Constance pulled the doors to the Throne Room closed. She smiled when she saw Lance coming down the stairs.

"Good day, Sir Lance. I trust you're feeling better after Lady Gwin's attentions."

Lance's throat constricted. Instead of an answer, he gave Lady Constance a quick bow. "My lady, I need you to open a ley line for me."

"Oh?" she said peering at the healed wound on his arm.

"My wound is healed. I have urgent business to tend to."

"Well, certainly I can open a line for you." Lady Constance reached for the door handle of the Throne Room, but she paused before opening it. "I'm only surprised Lady Gwin isn't here to do it for you."

"She's tending to her husband." Those words dumped cold water down on his head. It was the sensation he needed to cool any more of his wayward thoughts about Gwin.

"Where are you going?" Lady Constance asked.

"Champagne, France. To the de Payens House."

"I thought that manse was deserted?"

"It is. But I need to check out a lead there."

And while checking on the lead regarding Malegant, Lance could put some distance between himself and Gwin. He needed the time and the space to come to grips with what had happened between them and to ensure that it never happened again.

10

Gwin searched the entire castle, from the dungeons to the Weapons Room, to the training fields, to the stables. She couldn't find Lance. She'd never sought him out purposefully, but still, she'd always managed to bump into him.

The two had been like magnets the entire time they'd been in each other's lives. She would always look up and see him not too far. The few times in her life that she had been in danger, he'd stepped in front of her. Now, when she ached to be in his arms, he was nowhere to be found.

She knew he hadn't gone shopping with Morgan and Arthur. Mainly because she knew Arthur was preoccupied—dragging his fiancée bodily on the errand. But also because she'd texted Morgan who had already left and said Lance wasn't with them.

He wasn't out with Tristan and Percy. Gwin had checked the town's group chat and there was no mention or tagging of Lance in the posts. He wasn't with the remaining squires in their little gaming hole. Gwin had ventured in there under the guise of needing to replace a broken controller, and there had been no sign of Lance.

In a moment of desperation, she'd even been so bold as to go to his rooms and knock on the door. A place she'd never been to in the century he'd lived in the castle. But when she knocked on his door, there was no response.

Where could he have gone?

He'd been there every time she'd needed him. Was he avoiding her now? Had he not wanted to kiss her? What if he did have someone else?

It had been a century since she'd turned from the feelings they shared. He'd moved on, of course, he had. She'd never seen any evidence of it. Lance was too much a gentleman to ever flaunt it in her face.

Still, she knew there were others. How could there not be? Lance was young and virile ... and available. Unlike her.

Gwin was still shackled to the mistake she'd made a century ago. Now that she was turning the key and freeing herself from that lock, it was too late.

What had she expected? That he'd kept himself pure for her, for decades. It was a ridiculous notion. Especially when, by all accounts, she hadn't waited for him.

What would he think when he found out the truth about her? That she still carried her V-card, as Loren would call it. What if the thought turned him off?

She was ancient by human standards of counting, but she was in her prime as a witch. All women her age had experience. Lance would likely not want a fumbling, untried virgin. Would he?

She didn't know? The world looked different to her now that she'd tasted Lance's lips. Now that she'd been held in his embrace. Now that she'd made the decision that they would be together.

Because they would. Be together. No matter if he was seeing someone else.

Gwin knew in her heart that they were meant to be together. Hell, everyone knew it. And whoever this chit was that was in her way would step aside or get blasted by magic.

Gwin put her hand to her head. She was fevered.

That was the only explanation for those unkind, possessive thoughts. Though her thoughts had been unsavory, they hadn't been untrue.

She was certain Lance's feelings for her went beyond the chivalric. She knew his sense of duty didn't stop at protecting her. He had responded to that kiss. She knew he had. She knew he felt something. Didn't he?

"There you are."

Gwin looked up at the sound of her mother's voice. She thought her mother had gone with Morgan and Arthur. She thought she'd have a few hours' reprieve from her mother's way of coddling her daughters.

"I'm going to need your help with this wedding since your sister could give a care," said Gwynfhar. "She hasn't commissioned a new carriage to be built to cart them from the ceremony to the reception. She hasn't ordered gold ink for the invitations. And she hasn't even begun talking to any of the top designers in France or Italy for her gown."

"Because she doesn't want those things for her wedding."

Gwynfhar pressed her perfectly manicured fingers to her lace bodice. Her face was horror-stricken. "Of course she does. She just doesn't know it yet."

"Morgan and Arthur just want to be together."

"You're making my case. Morgan didn't think she wanted to marry Arthur when she was a girl. But look at her now."

True, Morgan hadn't wanted to marry Arthur when she was younger, even though her mother pushed her to it. Morgan had pushed back and enjoyed her life instead. And then, in the end, she and Arthur had found one another on their own terms.

Pride replaced the pinched look of horror on her mother's face. She had two girls who'd nabbed the royal blood of Camelot. The only difference was that Morgan was in love with her betrothed and he loved her in return.

Gwin wondered what her life would've been like if she hadn't succumbed to outside interference in her affairs of the heart. She would've married Lance. She'd probably have a gaggle of children tugging at her skirts. She'd have a man who would kiss her senseless. A man who would not hide when she went looking for him. Because that was the only explanation, he was hiding from her.

"Are you listening to me?"

Gwin's attention snapped back to her mother.

"We need to save that girl from herself. She doesn't know what she wants. Mother knows best."

Gwin knew her mother meant well. But Gwynfhar had it all wrong. Her mother never had a clue as to what was best for her daughters. Only what was best for her idea of Gwin's and Morgan's lives.

"Mother, I'm getting a divorce."

Gwynfhar's eyes grew as large and wide as an owl's. Her eyes narrowed to slits like a snake's. Then her head whipped around and away from Gwin's. She stormed down the hall, looking in doors and down dark corridors.

"Where is he?" Gwynfhar hissed.

"He? Who?" Gwin trailed after her. She'd seen her mother disapproving. She'd seen her mother upset. But this was something different.

"Where is that bastard?"

Gwin's teeth ground so hard she had to spit out a chipped piece of her molars before she could answer. "He is not a bastard. He is the most decent man I've ever known."

"Oh?" Her mother wheeled around, bringing Gwin up short. "What decent man would dally with a married woman?"

"He didn't ... I did. I kissed him."

Her mother drew back as though Gwin had slapped her.

"Mother, I've been so unhappy all these years with Merlin."

Gwin was hoping for compassion in her mother's gaze, but Gwynfhar only glared. Gwin didn't expect her mother to open her arms to her and welcome her into a hug. But she did want her mother to understand. Just as she was having trouble finding Lance, it looked like she wouldn't find what she was looking for in her mother either.

"You fool girl," said Gwynfhar. "Do you have any idea what this will do to your reputation?"

"I don't care." And she didn't. Just a year ago, Gwin would've been horrified at her words, at her behavior. But now, she wanted to shout from the rooftops that she loved Lance and wanted to be with him. "I want to be happy. Don't you want me to be happy?

When her mother didn't answer, Gwin decided to give up this fight and return to her original mission; the mission she should've embarked on over a century ago.

"Where are you going?" her mother called behind her.

"To find Lancelot."

The heels of Gwin's shoes impacted each stair in the Great Hall as she stepped down from on high. Her eyes blurred with her mother's silent rejection. That's why she didn't see the person coming toward her.

Gwin teetered as she crashed into Lady Constance. Constance put her hands out and then around Gwin until she was steady. Gwin was so starved for affection that she had the urge to collapse inside the woman's arms.

But she didn't. She straightened her spine and plastered on her Hostess Smile. Though she considered Constance a friend, this was not a conversation she wanted to have with the woman.

"I'm so sorry, Gwin," said Constance.

"No, it's my fault. I wasn't paying attention to where I was going."

"Did I hear you say you were looking for Lancelot?"

Gwin froze. How much of the conversation between herself and her mother had Constance heard? Gwin decided it didn't matter what Constance had heard. She knew where to find Lance.

"I opened a ley line for him not fifteen minutes ago."

"Where did he go?" Gwin asked.

"France."

Gwin looked over her shoulder. Her mother hadn't followed her down the stairs and was no longer at the top.

Good.

Because Gwin was going to do something her mother would certainly disapprove of. She was leaving behind her duty. She was following her heart. She would go to France, find Lance, and continue what she started in the infirmary.

11

The ley line to Champagne opened in the wine cellar of the manse. This particular ley line doorway wasn't built on a church or place of religious significance like most places where ley energies covered. Still, this home was hallowed ground.

The manse was once the home of Joseph of Arimathea, the uncle of the prophet Jesus. Arimethea's wife was Mary Magdalene, one of the most powerful witches the world had ever known.

Arthur, the first of his name, had married the daughter of Joseph and Mary. They raised their children in this home, including their grandson, Hugues de Paganis, also known as Hugo de Payens, the founder of the Knights Templar.

The house had been empty for nearly a year. The last tenant, an elderly witch who had looked after the place, had been drained of her power and left to die by Merlin when he'd gone on his rampage.

Just the thought of the wizard made Lance ill. What his poor Gwin had had to endure, bearing his touch for decades

No. He promised himself he'd never think of that. The problem was now that he'd tasted her lips, Lance couldn't not think of her.

It had seemed it was new to her, their kiss. Touching her lips to another, being held in an embrace. Had that bastard hurt her during their intimate moments?

Lance clenched his fists so hard he heard his bones splinter.

Wait. No. That wasn't bone. It was a floorboard. Someone was upstairs in the house.

Lance pulled his brooch from his shirt. He didn't unleash his sword as he stepped carefully up the stairs. Peeking into the entryway, he spotted a dozen Templars.

The men wore the modern white tunic with a red cross over the chest of the new world order. The crosses had hooks at the edges, unlike the original Templars whose crosses were two, simple straight lines. These men had clean-shaven faces, emoji hair, and in one case cowboy boots. Their appearance told Lance that these men were more modern than moral standard-bearers as the order called for. Half of them looked like comic con rejects while the other half looked like ninja warrior wannabes.

They were all human. The dangerous kind of human. They'd drunk the Kool-Aid of a zealot. That made them think they were heroes and righteous of a bad flavor.

A spindly man stepped forward. He looked no thicker than a sword. He reminded Lance of the allergy-prone scientist back in the infirmary. That must be Simon Accolon's father, Malegant. Lance doubted the man could lift a sword himself, which was likely why he got amateurs to do his dirty work.

Before he could decide what move to make, Lance felt a sharp point at his back. His shoulders slumped. Not out of resignation. Out of embarrass-ment that a toy soldier had snuck up and got the drop on him.

Lance slipped the brooch containing his sword onto his thumb and placed his hands up in the air in mock surrender.

"One of the knights of Camelot?" said the nasally

voice behind him. "They said you all were tough, but I caught you on my first night out."

The man sounded pleased with his prowess. Lance decided to let the kid believe he was in control for a while longer. With a shove, the Templar pushed Lance out of the door and into the awareness of the dozen men. The men stood in the library surrounded by ancient books lining wall to wall shelves. They'd taken a moment to light the fire, which was the only illumination in the room.

The other toy soldiers all immediately drew their swords. Lance was lucky they observed the sword fighting tradition of the original knights. If they used guns, like modern soldiers, bullets would've riddled the entire room with their nervous fingers.

"Look what I found, my lord," said the baby Templar.

Lance bit the inside of his mouth. The Templars who remained were not of noble lineage. They didn't deserve the honorific of *lord*, especially with the direction of their moral endeavors of killing harmless witches.

"Malegant, I presume," said Lance.

The man's smile was reminiscent of a cartoon villain. He just needed to twirl his greasy mustache. "I see my reputation precedes me."

"Actually, it's your son who gave me a description. He's being held captive in Camelot, by the way. I'm surprised you haven't mounted a rescue effort."

Malegant shrugged. "He chose his mom in the divorce. So, it serves him right."

Lance felt a momentary pang for the scientist. His own father would never have lifted a finger to save him either. Even when the sword chose him, his father couldn't bring himself to claim Lance.

In Lance's current predicament, the raised swords around him glinted in the lamplight. Lance remained calm and still. A rescue would be welcome, but not necessary. As long as he kept himself calm and alert, Lance would find a way out of this. It was just a dozen inept humans playing with sharp sticks.

"You're trespassing on private property," said Lance.

"De Payens was the founder of the Knights Templar. He laid the foundation for what our organization would become. We have every right to be here. It's you who are trespassing."

"This was his grandparents' home," said Lance. "Joseph of Arimathea and the witch Mary Magdalene."

The swords lowered incrementally as the play

knights looked around at each other. Confusion, disbelief, and wonder colored their faces in the low light. Except Malegant, whose face showed fury and indignation.

"Oh?" drooled Lance. "You didn't tell them?"

"That's blasphemy." The spittle collected at the corners of Malegant's mouth, settling on his pointy mustache. "More lies by you devils who dared to steal God's glory."

Templars believed magical kind stole their powers. Eve and the devil and the apple and such. The apple in the story being the source of magic. There was some truth to the made-up version. But no snake. No Adam either. Just a lost, hungry human girl in a realm of magic.

Lance kept his explanations to himself. He was more interested in Malegant's explanation of his doings. Lance had done the hero-villain thing enough that he knew if he kept quiet, the bad guy would spill his dastardly plan.

"This is what the Knights of Camelot do with their lies and their trickery. It's why the Templars were formed, to combat the magic that had broken loose on God's creatures. For centuries, magic has plagued God-fearing servants. Your spells have toppled crowns, crippled the church, and cursed armies. Your treachery even worked its way into our ranks, all the way to our last Grand Master. But now, in this day, we will reverse your curse on our order."

As villain speeches went, Lance was having trouble following the diatribe. The last Grand Master of the Templars? "Do you mean Jacques de Molay?"

"Of course you would know the name of the traitor," said Malegant. "He was one of your kind."

The Templars had been founded by the son of a witch, but its ranks were populated by devout humans. Those with magical blood became knights. Once again, Malegant had all of his facts wrong.

By the time the Templars' demise began, the order had long since broken with Camelot. It had come under the thumb of the church and crown.

"The wizard, de Molay, revealed himself and placed a curse on the Templars that fateful night of Friday the 13th. Many believed the curse was on the king and pope. It may have been as well. But the main curse was on the Templars. Hundreds of Templars were arrested across France. And while hundreds were jailed, burned, and killed, still hundreds of bodies were missing. Did you never wonder what happened to them?"

"No," said Lance. "It's the twenty-first century.

They're dead."

"Not dead. Sleeping."

Okay. Lance decided to upgrade this guy from villain to lunatic.

"Before the massacre, some of the Templars got away. There were rumors that they got word of de Molay's treachery and went into hiding."

It still made no sense to Lance. Even if some got away, it was still hundreds of years later. None of those men would have survived. Perhaps Malegant was talking about their descendants? Somehow, Lance doubted it.

"Legend has it they were cursed by de Molay and turned to stone."

"Uh huh," Lance nodded slowly, looking around at the pointed blades. He was no longer paying mind to Malegant and his insane ideas. He was plotting his inevitable escape. He kept talking only to humor the man. "You think Templars were turned to stone?"

"They were cursed. But now it's time for the Stone Templars to rejoin the new world order. I just need to find them. I believe the records were kept in one of the Grand Master's residences."

"You can't turn people to stone." He didn't think?

Now it was Malegant who nodded as though he

were humoring Lance. "Just like you can't pull a steel sword out of stone. Or shove a blade into a pen or a brooch. Or travel across space and time through magical doors."

Okay. He had him there. But those were magical objects, not beings. There was a clear, living, and breathing difference.

"Magic transforms you. Only God has that power, and you stole it. It's my job to return it. Starting with returning the lives you stole. I just need a little magic to reverse the spell. I wish I had a full-blooded witch or wizard instead of a half-blood bastard like you."

The calm and cool that Lance had collected fell away. "I really don't like that word."

Malegant shrugged. "It's what you are, isn't it? Sir Lancelot, son of a noble knight and a whore."

Lance knew he should take a deep breath and reach for reason. Twelve untried novices were dangerous in their unpredictability and potential for chaos. But that word was his button. That and Gwin. And the Gwin-button had already been pressed earlier. So, he had nothing to grasp onto.

Lance pushed on his brooch and unleashed his sword.

Twelve points aimed at him. Lance didn't want to

kill the men. They all likely had corporate or dead-end jobs to get back to on Monday. Templars were once brought up in the order. Not like these late-in-life converts who wanted to play adventure on the weekends.

Still, their swords were sharp and pointing at him. And just as he expected, they didn't come at him one or two at a time in an orderly fashion. They all lifted their heels to charge, wanting to pop their sword-fighting cherry. They'd do as much damage to each other as they would do to him with their eager lack of a plan. This would not end well for any of them.

Except Malegant who tactically moved out of range.

This was going to be a bloodbath and not one Gwin could heal him from. He'd run into battle to get away from the temptation of her. Now, the only way he'd see her again would be a miracle.

A Bible flew off one of the shelves, through the air, and thumped on one of the Templar's heads. Then another good book. Then another, each making perfect aim at a Templar's forehead.

Lance would've thought maybe God was on his side. Apparently, She was. As if pulled by magic, his gaze lifted, and there she was.

12

Gwin pulled more energy from the ley line and sent a third and fourth book flying. A thick tome thumped one of the men on his head, a scroll hit the back of another man's head. They both fell forward, knocked out cold.

That was four down. But there were still eight standing against Lance. However, the flying books had spooked the men, and they'd all lowered their swords as they whipped their heads left and right, trying to suss out where the danger was coming from.

She sent another thick book flying across the room.

Gwin's magic set off chasing the man around until it whacked him on the bottom and then across the head, sending him asleep along with the other four men.

The rest of the men looked around frantically at the ancient religious symbols about the room. By the fear on their faces, it was certain they believed judgment was upon them.

"It's a witch," said the man who'd backed away from all the fighting. His lanky frame resembled the young Simon Accolon who still slept in the infirmary back at the castle.

Lance's gaze found hers through the crack in the door. When it did, his sword lowered also. His once fierce expression turned horror-stricken at the sight of her. His chest heaved as though he'd been punched in his gut because he had.

"Double bubble toil and trouble. Come out or I'll poke your knight like a bubble."

With a nod from Malegant, the man who'd punched Lance in the gut turned his sword on Lance's neck. Gwin's life flashed before her eyes with the glint of that blade at Lance's neck.

Doubled over, Lance shook his head at her from where he spotted her in her hiding place in the ley line doorway. *Go home*, his eyes communicated with her. *Save yourself.*

Like hell, she would. Gwin stepped out of her

hiding spot. She put her hands up. She could still perform spells with her hands raised. It was only the blade at Lance's throat that kept her magic at bay.

"Get the abomination," said Malegant. "I'll need her magic to break the spell once we find the Stone Templars."

Lance stepped up to the blade, turning to place his body between hers and the rest of the men. His voice was filled with a menace she didn't know he was capable of. "You'll touch her over my dead body."

The big man dressed in a modern take on Templar garb shrugged "Fine by me."

Gwin saw red when blood pricked at Lance's neck just beside his bobbing Adam's apple. The skin broke, and her palms flared.

"Ah ah ah," tsked Accolon's father.

Gwin glared up at the man. There were still six Templars standing. Lady Gwin had never hurt another living soul, outside of the book thumping a moment ago. But seeing harm being inflicted on the man she loved pushed a button in her.

That was the last thing she thought as the big man flew up and against the wall. The hard crack was sickening. She was certain she'd broken something with the force of her magic. She didn't care.

Hostess Gwin had left the building. Get Along To Go Along Gwin was nowhere to be found.

Her attention turned to the man coming toward her with a sword raised. She'd never had anyone approach her with aggression in her entire life. Other than her husband. But he always launched foul words, not a fist or sword.

The magic she had employed to lift and toss the big man had taken a lot from her. She reached down, pulling more energy from the abundant ley energy running under the ancient house. She raised her hands to ward off her next attacker, only to have warm blood splatter across her palms.

Lance's blade struck down the advancing Templar. Lance's gaze connected with hers. His blue eyes blazed with fury. Gwin shrank back from the rage that curled his lips.

She blinked, trying to wipe the sight of Lance's malice from her view. When she opened her eyes again, Lance had turned from her. His sword made figure eights, slicing the torsos of two more men before she could even catch her breath.

There was nothing for her to do but watch. He'd drawn all attention from her to him. With the last four men standing, Lance moved easily, disarming the men who outnumbered him. None of them outmanned him.

A loud crash sounded from behind her when the last of the four men fell. She felt heat at her back. Gwin turned into a blaze that lit the room. Somehow, the fire had escaped the confines of the fireplace.

She saw how. Malegant held vintage bottles of wine in his two palms. He must've grabbed them from the cellar. Gwin felt a moment of anger that he'd destroy the priceless vintages.

Lance backed his body toward Gwin, offering her protection as fire engulfed the room and blocked them from the cellar doorway and the ley line. They looked up to see Malegant and a couple of the bruised Templars exiting the room.

"I thought we needed the witch," said the big Templar, who Gwin had launched against the wall.

"Leave her," said Malegant. "I'll get another by the time we find the Stone Templars."

The door slammed behind the escaping Templars. Gwin heard something heavy fall down on the other side. With both exits blocked or up in flames, there was no way out.

She couldn't extinguish the fire without water nearby. She could use her magic to send the fire somewhere, but there was no exit. They were trapped. But they were together.

Lance pulled her to him. She went willingly. If it was going to end, this was the way she wanted to go, in his arms. But he wasn't pulling her into his arms.

Lance took Gwin's hand and tugged her to the far side of the room. He wasn't gazing lovingly into her eyes. He was looking up.

There was a high window. He tossed his sword up. The blade hit the glass and the window smashed, raining down shards of glass. Once again, Lance used his body to shield hers from the downpour.

Lance straightened and lifted Gwin in his arms. He hefted her up. She reached up, grasping the windowsill with her fingertips. Gwin lifted herself up and over the window. It was a long way down. Far enough that she could hurt herself if she didn't land well. A second later, Lance joined her as flames moved to follow.

Without hesitating, Lance wrapped her in his arms. He flung them toward the ground, angling his body so that he hit the ground first. Through his body, Gwin felt the impact and it stole her breath.

They stayed on the ground for the briefest of seconds. Then they were up. Lance swooped up his sword in one arm and her in the other. And then they were running.

Their escape wasn't soon enough. The fire raced up the side of the house faster than Lance's feet could carry them. The explosion shook the earth.

They went airborne. Lance caught Gwin's body again, in mid-air this time. Wrapping himself around her, they fell again to the ground. She felt no impact, only his body cushioning hers.

This time, instead of holding still for a second, they rolled. She was light as she landed on his chest but then felt him crush her as she reeled over and beneath him. On and on it went. Until finally, they came to a crashing halt in a ditch. Even when they came to a stop she was still cradled in his body.

Lance lifted his head, glaring down at her. The anger and fury that had been directed at the Templars were now aimed squarely at her.

"What are you doing here?" he shouted, his chest heaving.

"I-I needed to find you."

"I'm on a quest."

"I ... I ..."

"You could've been killed."

"I saved your life."

"That is not your job." He reared up, crowding

over her. "You're not a knight. You have no training. You don't belong here. Your place is in the castle. It's in your job title; Lady of the Castle. Not Lady of the Quest."

The shock of him yelling wore off quickly. She felt her muscles quiver as the tension built. The flush of heat that swept through her was not one of desire.

Gwin opened her mouth, preparing to raise her voice right back at Lance. She wasn't sure what she was going to say. She'd never know because a dark figure moved in the distance. The figure didn't move toward them. But she could feel the menacing energy reaching toward them. Her hackles raised as the figure's arm did.

Gwin grabbed Lance and pulled him down. She rolled with him deeper into the ditch as the bullets whizzed past his head. Down in the crevice of the earth, Lance stared at her. His blue eyes shining brighter than the stars in the night. He shut his mouth as they heard the slam of a car door and then the tear of tires.

13

The sound of car doors slamming and tire wheels screaming at the asphalt didn't assuage Lance's pounding heart. His limbs tingled as they crouched over Gwin's body. Inside, he felt his organs quivering with anxiety.

First the blades, then the fire, then the bullets. She could've died three different ways tonight. His stomach churned at the very thought of it.

He had no care that the blade had pierced his skin. Even now blood dripped down his neck. He didn't think twice about the ruined skin of his wrists where the fire had bit at him. He had no concern that a bullet came close to launching into his skull and knocking his mortal lights out. His only thought was for Gwin's safety.

That's why Lance remained over Gwin longer than was prudent. He covered her body with his to keep any more danger at bay. His body only barely touched hers, but where it did he felt a flame hotter than the fire that consumed the manse.

Even though he was battered, burned, and bruised, his body felt alive. He told himself it was the adrenalin, that it was the magic. But he knew it was all because of her.

He had her in his arms, exactly the opposite of his intentions when coming here. Nothing had gone right tonight. The bad guy had got away. But Lance had gotten more information.

Gwin was safe. Unfortunately, they had no quick escape with the ley line door gone. Malegant, and what was left of his weak army, could spot them easily if they took the road. The two of them were sitting ducks.

He had to get her out of here. But he had to let her go first. Slowly, carefully, reluctantly, Lance lifted himself off of Gwin.

He crouched low as he rose, surveying the area for danger. The house burned in the moonlight. The road was bare without tail or headlights. He saw movement in the distance. It was the four-legged variety. Just what he needed.

He extended his offering down to Gwin. But she didn't take his hand. Her eyes glistened in the night. His heart stopped.

"Are you hurt?"

She couldn't be wounded. God couldn't be so cruel. He'd done everything in his power to keep her out of harm and take the brunt of every assault that had neared her.

"Yes," she whispered.

Her voice was so small, so frail. It pierced Lance everywhere the Templar blades had failed to penetrate. He crouched down over her, searching for her wound.

"Where?" he demanded.

"My heart."

Lance looked down at her chest. There was no blood. He put his hand on her chest. Her heartbeat was steady. In fact, the beats increased.

Their gazes connected.

He and Gwin didn't get to share many words in their life. She could communicate with just a blink of her eyes how she felt. She didn't blink now. A single tear seeped from the corner of her right eye.

Lance caught it with his thumb. With the tear shed, her emotions were clear on her face. Looking into her eyes, Lance saw the same feelings in his soul reflected back at him.

It had always been plain for all to see that there was something between them. The only difference tonight was that Gwin wasn't fighting it any longer. She wasn't holding her feelings at bay. Why?

"Is he dead?" Lance asked. He tried to keep the hope from his voice. He was certain he failed.

"Who?"

"Your husband."

"No."

Lance shut his eyes. He pulled his hand from her heart. He lifted his body from hers.

Gwin sat up. "Why do you keep doing that? Why do you keep turning away from me? I finally open myself up to you and you treat me like a pariah. You yell at me for saving your life. Lance, if there's someone else, if you don't care for me any longer, just say so."

"If I don't care for …?"

He stood now. He was backlit by the burning house. If there was anyone about other than the agitated livestock moving away from the house, he'd be an easy target.

"You kissed me in front of your dying husband

and a stranger. You hid me behind a curtain like something to be ashamed of."

"A curtain?"

Lance regrouped, getting back on track. "I knew I wasn't good enough to marry you. But I never expected you to treat me like a bastard."

"No." She let the word out in a rush. "You know I don't feel that way about you."

She also stood. The two of them casting long shadows on the ground as the flames licked up to the roof.

"I love you," she shouted. "I've always loved you."

Her words didn't surprise him. They soothed his weary heart to hear out loud, finally. But like an aspirin, it only offered temporary relief to an underlying ailment.

"Yes," he nodded. "In the pure way, in the chivalric way. Your love is the best thing about me. Please don't ever sully it with offers of adultery and secret kisses."

Her eyes widened in shock. Guilt dampened her lashes. Shame glittered in those irises.

For the first time in a long time, Lance felt like a bastard. Watching the torrid emotions play across Gwin's face confirmed that she had acted out of love and not lust. She was not like the widows and wanton wives of Camelot.

Lance reached out and tilted her chin up so that she met his gaze. He let his heartbeat resonate in his gaze. Her gaze begged forgiveness. He brushed a few more tears away until he was certain she saw his absolution.

Lance held out his hand again. "Please, let me get you to safety."

Gwin took his hand. He wrapped his palm around hers and allowed her warmth to run a course through his blood. Once she completed her invasion, Lance cursed himself. He could've gotten much closer. She could be in his arms, instead of just connected to his palm. He could've kissed her again.

But that wasn't who they were.

Retracing their steps back to the complacent companionship they'd shared for decades, they walked the fields in silence. The path they were on looked different than it had in the past. Lance knew the right thing was to let her go.

He'd done his duty. She was not in immediate danger. His next obligation was to get her back home. The closest ley line was in Paris, a far cry from Champagne. Luckily, their ride pranced in front of them.

Letting Gwin go, Lance held up his hands to approach the stallion. The horse eyed him warily. "Might I beg a ride for myself and the lady?"

The horse neighed and reared up on its hind legs. Lance took a few steps back, making sure to keep Gwin behind him. But looking back, he saw that she had rounded him and was approaching the horse.

The dark stallion bowed its head in clear deference to the lady. It was clear that the two of them were communicating, leaving Lance out of the discussion. The horse was of the magical breed that had been brought to Europe centuries ago by the first knights. The ley energy had enabled the horses to communicate with other magical beings.

Lance had to assume that since these horses had been on lands without knights for decades, they were out of practice. But it would seem they still had their manners when it came to ladies.

The horse bobbed its head, as though it were agreeing to Gwin's request. It lifted one of its front legs allowing her to step up and swing her body over its back. They both turned to Lance.

Lance swung his body up and over the horse. It was a snug fit on the broad stallion's back as his groin rested against Gwin's backside.

It was going to be a long ride to Paris.

14

Gwin had been an avid rider her entire life. But, over the course of her life, her horses only ever strolled her around the castle. She rarely had occasion to gallop. Ladies weren't meant to be jostled, said her mother. So, Gwin spent her life atop a horse moving at a trot.

The wild steed from Champagne ran at top speeds through the French countryside. The magical stallions which had come over from the Holy Lands centuries ago and settled in places of great ley energy easily reached one hundred miles per hour. The stallion that carried them, Meginhard the steed said his name was, flew beyond that.

The pins flew out of Gwin's hair, leaving it streaming behind her like a blonde flag in the black night. She leaned forward, burying her hands and her nose in the steeds flowing curtain of dark hair. The strength, the scent, the feel of the horse should've been her only thoughts.

They weren't.

The press of leather-clad legs boxing her in from either side made her pulse race. The muscled arms holding her tight stole her breath. The defined abdomen at her back sent heat rushing down to her seat.

Lance consumed Gwin's every thought, her every inhale, her every exhale, her every twitch, and even her stillness. In the stillness of her mind, his words played over again in her mind.

Your love is the best thing about me. Please don't ever sully it with offers of adultery and secret kisses.

She took care of everyone around her. She prided herself on knowing their needs better than they did. How had she not anticipated what her words and actions would do to Lance?

He was the person she most cared for, the one she paid the most attention to. And she had hurt him deeply, carelessly, selfishly.

She knew there were still some in their community who thought ill of him for his parentage. A matter that he'd had no control over. A non-issue that he had risen above to become the best knight in all of Camelot.

And she'd denigrated his character with that kiss and her offer of what? Adultery. Because that was all she could offer him while she was still married.

Even now his sadness choked her. She wanted to turn and embrace him, but she knew it wouldn't be received well. So, she held stiff in his protective embrace as they rode into the night.

They were headed to Paris, where the closest access to a ley line was located. Paris was about 150 kilometers from Champagne. They reached the city lights of Paris in just under three hours under the horsepower of the magical steed.

The sun was just beginning to stretch its rays after a good night's sleep when Lance hopped off the horse's back. He reached up for Gwin. Her limbs were stiff and instead of landing straight down, her body crashed into his.

The feel of his hard chest against her softness made her breath catch. He gasped as well and his hot breath hit her hard. She held onto him as her knees buckled. When she looked up, their lips were close.

Everything in her urged her to close the distance between them and capture his mouth with hers.

Her gaze rose to meet his. In his eyes, Gwin saw turmoil.

Desire mixed with despair. Hunger mixed with shame. Indecision mixed with certainty.

She made the decision for them both. "I'm so sorry," she said stepping away from him.

"Gwin," he started and then stopped. He ran his hands through his hair in frustration. "I need to get you to safety," he said finally.

She understood. He was retreating to duty. It's what she would've done in his position. It's what she was doing now. Focusing on his comfort instead of her own.

They walked the empty streets of the most romantic city in the world in silence. They moved side by side. Lance walked on the side closest to the street even though only a few cars were in gear. As they moved farther into the city, the streets became peopled with workers and health enthusiasts out for a jog. Those people stared at them with dismay, some crossing to the other side of the street.

Gwin scanned both herself and Lance to understand why. Their clothes were muddied and torn from the fight, the fire, and the ride.

"We can't get into Notre Dame looking like this," she said.

Their destination was the church which held an active ley line that would lead them back home. They walked a bit more until they came to a market. Lance stopped her with a hand at her low back. No sooner than his fingertips touched her did he jerk his hand away as though she'd scalded him.

Lance ducked behind a row of clothes leaving her alone, but still within his sight. Gwin stayed where he'd left her and watched him interact with the saleswoman.

Lance emerged from the rows of racks with a pair of women's jeans and a blouse. He held the garments out to her as though they were meant for her.

Gwin looked doubtful. Modern day clothing was made one size fits all unlike the fitted dresses of her time. It wasn't likely that these jeans would fit.

But she humored him. Perhaps they could laugh at the ill fit when she emerged. Perhaps that would settle them back on the road to an easy camaraderie.

She ducked into a washing room, splashed water on her face. Used soap from the dispenser, and paper towels to clean what she could. She felt almost human, which wasn't saying much since she was a witch.

She slipped into the jeans. She was surprised to

find that the garment fit her perfectly. When she went shopping with her sister and Loren, they'd spend hours trying to find the perfect garment. But Lance had done it in only five minutes.

She emerged from the bathroom to find Lance was waiting for her. He'd tugged on a clean shirt and was scrubbing his face with the ruined cloth of his old shirt.

"You can go and wash up if you'd like," said Gwin.

He gave a gruff shake of his head. "I'll not leave you alone."

"I'm a witch and not some helpless damsel."

"Witches can't dodge bullets. One nearly got you." He tensed, as though the memory materialized and socked him on the chin. "Never do that again."

"I won't." She ached to reach out to him, wanting, needing to comfort him.

"If a bullet or a blade comes between you and me, promise me you'll never step in front of it."

She frowned, trying to make sense of his words. "No. I'll never promise you that. If ever your life is in my hands, I'll do whatever is necessary to save it."

"Your life is worth more than mine."

"Not by my calculations."

"Gwin—"

"I won't hear any more of this. You carry this false belief that you're not worth much. It's the falsest thing I've ever known. You are the best man I know. You're entirely selfless, unendingly caring. And you have a surprising knack for choosing women's clothing. You're a treasure."

That last comment accomplished what a caress or a hug would not. It loosened the knot of anxiety within them both. It cracked the corner of both of their mouths into a smile. It pushed forth gasps of humor from their lips.

"You've always had my good opinion," Gwin continued. "You'll never lose it. Please forgive me for hurting your pride and your honor. It was not my intention. I just ... It was selfish of me. I was thinking only of myself, my desires. I'm so, so sorry, Lance."

"I love you."

They were just three little words, but they flooded her with a warmth that witch fire could never rival. The hands that ached a second ago to reach out to him clutched at her belly as she held her breath waiting for his next words, his next move.

Please let his next move be with his mouth on hers. But Lance didn't move. He held his ground and spoke logically.

"That's not a shock. You've always known that.

Everyone knows that. But we both took vows. I'll not break my word. It may not be how we wanted to live our lives. But we'll do what we must. We won't be brought into temptation. You have my heart. You have my sword. You don't need my body."

"Right ..." She tried to nod her head, but it wobbled.

"We've always had a connection on a spiritual level. We have no need of the physical."

"No ..." Gwin shoved the word past her throat, but to her ears, it came out as a croak.

"I hate him."

She knew Lance referred to Merlin. But she was beginning to wonder, if it wasn't Merlin barring them from one another, would it always be something else standing in their way?

"I hate him for what he did to you all these years, for the terror he brought to this community. But I won't allow the poison of wishing him dead to seep into my heart. I saw you save him. I understand why you did it. You're not that person."

She shook her head. "No, I'm not."

"I would never want you to be anything or anyone but who you are."

"Lance." She gazed up at him, this man who owned her soul. "I love you, too."

"I know."

He held out his arm for her. She slipped her fingers into the crook of his elbow. She pressed her shoulder to his. Her head brushed his shoulder cap. Her hand slid down his bicep. Her fingers rested at the fleshy part of his palm just below his wrist. And then she captured his fingers in hers. Somehow, she felt like the captive.

A week ago this would be scandalous. A day ago it would've been enough. As the sun rose on this new day, it was a beginning. One that Gwin was determined to end with new vows; vows that would bring their hearts, their souls, and their bodies together.

But for this moment, it would be enough.

15

The Knights' Code came with the expectation that men, and now women, show strength in violent combat, but also steadfastness in the delicate manners of the court when they were off the battlefield. In Lance's estimation, the battlefield of marque floors was a far more treacherous place than a war zone.

He walked with Gwin down a stony path in the heart of Paris while conflict clashed inside of him. He loved her, that was as true as the sun gave warmth. But the rest of the words he'd just uttered to her were lies.

He could give a flying fig tree about his courtly vows. The Knights' Code could go hang itself on a tree. This woman held his heart. She consumed his spirit. He needed to give her his body. Right now he could only give her his arm.

The pads of Gwin's fingertips curled into his flesh, pushing the stake of their claim deeper into his person. The brush of her shoulder against his was enough to knock him down. The sensation of her thigh against his, even in the jeans that molded her trim legs, made his knees want to buckle and bend to her earlier request.

She wanted him. Not just carnally. She wanted a life with him.

The problem was that it would be a love in the dark, and he would not go there. He would not go into a locked room, or behind a closed curtain, or run off into a distant land like his father had with his mother. No, he would not bring that shame on either of them. Now, if her bastard of a husband died ...

"A charm for your wife, sir?" A street vendor inserted himself in their path. His thick French accent lacing his English words.

Lance's hand was on his brooch, ready to release his sword before the man rolled the R in "sir." Lance faltered at the question mark. His finger fumbled on his weapon at the word the man had used to describe Gwin.

Gwin's eyes were fastened to the piece of

costume jewelry. Her fingers dug into his bicep. He wasn't sure what had thrilled her. The title the salesman gave her or the trinket he offered.

Lance pulled out his wallet. The Euros he found inside were crisp at the edges. In a century, he'd never had occasion to present a trinket of his affection to his lady. Though every battle had been won in her honor.

Sliding the cheap bracelet over her fingers and onto her wrist felt like he was making an oath. The look in her eyes let him know that she felt the same and that she made the pledge to him as well.

"Are you honeymooning in Paris?" asked the street vendor, holding up more wares, hoping to make another sale.

Gwin didn't answer. She turned to Lance and awaited his response. Hope glittered in her gaze.

"We're just passing through," Lance said. "We're on our way home."

Gwin's face fell at the hard truth.

Lance tucked her hand in his elbow, the bracelet rolling against his skin. He turned them on their way.

They walked aimlessly in the market for a few moments. The sun was high enough that Notre Dame would be open now. It was about a thirty-minute walk to the gothic cathedral. Lance knew the Templars couldn't have followed so quickly if they were even headed this way. Still, he'd relax once Gwin was back in the safety of the fortified magical castle of Camelot.

"Why do I feel so much ley energy here?" asked Gwin. "Are we close to Notre Dame?"

"This is Carreau du Temple. There was a Templar site here before progress overrode it."

"Do you believe any of what Malegant said? About de Molay?"

"That a Grandmaster of the Templar Order was a wizard? That he was working for our side?"

Gwin shrugged, her shoulder blade pressed into his forearm. "It's possible. A lot of knowledge was lost between Camelot and the Templars during that time. It was hard to know who to trust."

Lance had been born far after that time period. But he'd heard many of the old knights speak of their time when they fought beside the Templars and then how things changed.

"But it's not possible to turn a person to stone," said Lance.

Gwin didn't immediately respond. "I'm not so certain of that. Most myths have their basis in truth.

There are stories of Medusa whose power was petrification, turning men to stone."

"She's not real. We've met the Olympians."

Last year, the Lady of the Lake, Vivian, had swum off and married the Greek God Poseidon. Vivi and Psi were living happily in Athens. Psi kept the former merlady plied with designer shoes, leaving her to never want to jump into the water again.

Gwin's hand slid down Lance's forearm. Their wrists bumped. He caught her fingers with his. He told himself it was for her protection. He was certain he set a record for breaking his vow of candor in a single day.

"What about the stories of stone circle maidens?" she said. "Just about every culture that has stone formations have these tales of girls being punished for dancing on the Sabbath, or accused of witchcraft, or running off with a lover ..."

Gwin bit her lower lip and looked away from him. But she did not let his arm go. In fact, she squeezed him tighter as though she were afraid he'd slip through her fingers, or that she would be turned to stone for committing a few of those sins.

"It's funny how it's always the woman who gets punished in these stories," she said.

Lance had no response. His mind was far too

focused on the five fingers wrapped around his bicep and the other five laced with his fingers. His only thought was that a life of stone would be a worthwhile punishment for these stolen hours with the woman he loved.

16

———

The flying buttress of Notre Dame Cathedral rose into the dawning sky. The doors would be opening at any moment. Although closed doors were no deterrent to a knight and a witch. A few blocks away from the holy place, Gwin felt magic underfoot. There was also the ghost of something dark and hopeless, filled with great suffering.

Gwin knew some of the stories of the Templars. Those tales were mainly of their demise. She did remember the story of the Friday the 13th Massacre.

"This is where they burned them?" she said.

"No," said Lance. "It was done on the Seine. They were tortured, then burned, then drowned in the river."

"Burned and drowned? That's typically what humans do to witches."

A breeze unsettled her hair. Gwin felt the goose-flesh on her arms raise.

Lance had been right back in Champagne. Magic could not raise the dead. However, objects, places, and beings held onto magical energy long after the container began to decay. The Seine, the place of Grand Master Jacques de Molay's demise, wasn't that far away.

France had a relatively low rate of accusation and execution when it came to witchcraft. So what had happened here? What was the source of this energy she felt? Could some of the Templars who perished have had magical blood?

Lance gave her a tug, urging her toward the cathedral and the ley line that would take her home.

Gwin held back. She opened herself and listened closely to the magic underfoot. There was so much suffering in the trace of the past. She couldn't stand to see anything or anyone suffer and not do anything about it.

"Gwin, it's time to go home."

"There has to be more to this story," she said.

"Don't tell me you believe Malegant?"

"Not entirely. But what if there were wizards in

the Templar Order? They began under the guidance of the son of a witch. What if there were more magical offspring in the ranks?"

"We would've known that. There would've been records."

"Precisely. There must be a record of the origins of the Templars who perished."

"If there is, we'll come back and find it."

"But we're already here," she said. "We can pop into a hall of records or a university's library."

"I'll not keep you out in danger any longer."

"It's a library. What harm would that do?"

"Your sister nearly had her soul taken from her body at a college not too long ago."

"Please. I want to help." She also wasn't ready for her time alone with Lance to end. Before he could cut her off, she looked up and saw her salvation. "The Abbey Bookshop. Surely they'll have some history books I could peek inside. It would just be a few moments."

Lance looked to her, then to the side where the bookstore was situated, then over at the cathedral, and finally back to her. The journey already had his head moving in the negative. "I need to get you back home. Everyone will be beside themselves with worry."

"Then you can call them and let them know we're fine and that we're doing a little recon."

"Recon?"

"Please? Just a little longer?" She laid her hand on his chest, right over his beating heart. It was a bold move, but she was bolder now. Now that she knew the time they could be together was within reach.

She could see in his eyes that he knew she wasn't just talking about finding more facts. She wanted a little more time alone with him before they had to go back to their roles, back to their separate corners, back to not touching unless one of them was hurt.

The tension in his jaw released. "Enough time to make the phone call."

Gwin bounced on her toes. Lance tried and failed to hide the small smile that played across his lips at her happiness.

He led her into the bookstore. Still arm in arm. The smell of must and aged paper hit Gwin as the bell tinkled over the shop door.

They approached the reference desk. Gwin asked for directions to the ancient records on the Knights Templars. She was delighted to see they had a sizable corner.

Lance asked to use the shop's phone and the

pretty clerk allowed him in the "No Customers Beyond This Point" area with a toothy smile and a flip of her hair. As Lance passed the clerk, as he picked up the phone, as he placed it to his ear, his gaze never unlocked from Gwin.

Satisfied that she had Lance's attention over the clerk, Gwin turned her mind to the old books. The tomes didn't look ancient. But when she pulled one down and opened it, the writing inside of the new bindings was ancient.

Gwin bent her head down over the book in her hands. As if pulled by an invisible force, her fingers leafed through the pages and settled on one entry. The entry was for Jacques de Molay, the last Grand Master of the Templars.

The entry began at the man's beginning. He was born in a French territory that had been ruled by the Holy Roman Empire. His family was of minor nobility. De Molay was dubbed a knight at the age of twenty-one in the Chapel of Beaune Commandery. Shortly after his knighting, he went to the East.

There was little record of his life for twenty years during those times. Until he became Grand Master.

How did he make such a leap from provincial knight to the leader of the entire order?

Gwin looked up to see that Lance was still on the

phone. His gaze still locked on her, but his expression was pinched. Arthur or possibly even her mother must be giving him an earful. More reason she was not ready to go back home. If she found something important she might be able to prolong their adventure even more.

Looking back down into the pages, she saw that there was an attempt at a merger between the Templars and the Knights Hospitaller. The move appeared to be pushed by the Papacy. The pressure urged the leadership of the Templars to also merge with other military orders of the day and be placed under the authority of one king. But de Molay declined any attempts at mergers.

The readings told of how de Molay aimed to reform the Order during the waning days of the crusades. In de Molay's time, the Order had amassed great wealth, which King Philip and Pope Clement had their eyes on. The world knew how this story ended; with a bloody massacre on a Friday morning.

The next page was a transcript of de Molay's speech on the day of his death.

. . .

t is just that, in so terrible a day, and in the last moments of my life, I should discover all the iniquity of falsehood, and make the truth triumph. I declare, then, in the face of heaven and earth, and acknowledge, though to my eternal shame, that I have committed the greatest crimes but it has been the acknowledging of those which have been so foully charged on the order. I attest - and truth obliges me to attest - that it is innocent! I made the contrary declaration only to suspend the excessive pains of torture, and to mollify those who made me endure them. I know the punishments which have been inflicted on all the knights who had the courage to revoke a similar confession; but the dreadful spectacle which is presented to me is not able to make me confirm one lie by another. The life offered me on such infamous terms, I abandon without regret.

he transcriber told that the Grand Master spoke these words while standing on a platform over the Seine. On the scaffold of his death, de Molay had cursed his accusers, the King and the Pope.

King Philip and Pope Clement died within the

year. Curses were a dark magic not practiced in Camelot. Just because men died didn't necessarily mean de Molay was secretly a wizard.

What was interesting was the words of de Molay's curse. They were spoken in Latin and also in Arabic.

Gwin's Latin was a bit rusty. Her Arabic was a bit better since it was frequently spoken by the elderly in Camelot who'd either come from or spent time in the Holy Lands of the East. These words on the page could possibly be a curse. If de Molay had magical blood.

The sun shone through the window of the bookstore. Gwin scrubbed her eyes. She leaned back, rolling her head.

She needed to learn more about de Molay and his background. After reading his biography, she knew just the place to do it. Now she just needed to convince her escort to take a detour before they went home.

17

*L*ance kept his eye on Gwin as the phone rang. He ignored the shop clerk as she loosened a button on her blouse and leaned over, allowing her cleavage a freedom he wasn't interested in. Lance instead looked at the buttoned-up lady bent over a musty book. The shop was mostly empty at this time of day, but he trusted no one and no thing when it came to her safety.

He looked from the door of the shop to the table where Gwin sat. Her head was buried in the book. Her blonde hair spilled over her shoulders. She brushed it aside with a hand. He knew that expression. It was her determined expression.

She was determined to solve the mystery of the Stone Templars. The problem was the riddle amounted to the ravings of a madman. A madman that was still on the loose and could likely be headed toward this very city.

The thought of Malegant or one of his ill-trained goons getting their hands on Gwin again had Lance's hands balled into fists. He heard a crack and noted that he was near to destroying the phone in his hand. He had to get her home and quick.

He turned his attention back to the phone. He braced himself after the first ringing. He was certain he'd hear a gruff tone, demanding, filled with accusations and disappointment at his actions of having a lady out all night in his presence.

He cared that the reputation he'd work so hard to keep spotless would be tarnished. But it was nothing to the idea of him ruining Gwin's immaculate image. His shellacking would have to wait because the phone rang and then rang some more.

Until finally, a grumpy lion roared into the receiver. "What?"

Arthur answered on the fifth ring, which was unlike him. There was anger in Arthur's voice, but the tone sounded more like a roar of annoyance that the King of the Jungle had been roused from his rest and not the worry that one of his subjects had been out all hours of the night.

So, he hadn't been up all night with worry?

"I'm sorry I didn't call sooner," said Lance. "I lost my phone somewhere between the house fire in Champagne and the ride to Paris. This is the first chance I've had to call."

"Who is this?" Arthur growled.

Had he misdialed? But no, Lance was certain of the numerical code he'd dialed. And that was Arthur's deep voice, though not filled with the usual perceptiveness and alertness of his leader.

"It's Lancelot. Tall, redhead. Good with a sword. Your second in command."

"Who is it, Arthur?" came a feminine voice.

Lance recognized Morgan's voice. Though Arthur and Morgan hadn't taken their official marriage vows, they lived their lives as husband and wife day and night.

"We're sorry we've worried you," Lance began. "But we're both fine."

"Worry?" said Arthur.

"We?" said Morgan. Lance could hear her ruffling in the background. She'd likely pressed her ear to the phone so that she could hear too.

"What *we* are worrying me?" said Arthur.

Lance looked down at the receiver. Maybe Arthur and Morgan had stayed in last night, instead of going out? If so, then they wouldn't know that Gwin and Lance had left the castle.

Arthur had always had a Do Not Disturb rule when he was in his private quarters. No one dared approach the wing now that Morgan had moved into the lord's bedroom.

But surely word would have reached him by now. If not from Percy and Tristan, then at least from Gwin's mother who would want to move heaven and earth to save her daughter's reputation from the likes of Lance. Unless no one realized they were gone.

Only Lady Constance knew where Lance had gone last night because she'd opened the ley line for him. Gwin must've have run into Lady Constance to know where he was. If Lady Constance had told no one else, then it was entirely conceivable that no one knew and any potential scandal could be subdued.

"Me and Gwin," said Lance. "We're in Paris."

"So that kiss worked!" came Morgan's excited voice from much closer, as though she had taken the phone from Arthur.

"Kiss?" said Arthur from a little farther away, the sleep crumbled from his voice to be replaced by the perceptive alertness Lance was used to. "You kissed Gwin?"

Lance pulled the phone away from his ear at the

booming resonance of his leader. The shock wave of Arthur's bellow slapped Lance in the face. "She was in shock."

"She's married," said Arthur.

"Shut it," said Morgan. "The two of them belong together. It's finally their time."

"After her husband dies and sufficient time has passed," said Arthur. "We have to keep traditions."

"Oh?" said Morgan. "Like the tradition of having your fiancée, who's not yet your wife, in your bed?"

"That's different."

"How?"

"I gave you my vow."

"You think Lance didn't give his heart to Gwin a century ago. You think he stuck around here for duty? Everything that man does, every battle, every quest, every mission he's ever endured, he did for my sister."

In the resulting silence, Lance wished he could reach through the phone and kiss Morgan. Though that would've gotten him truly throttled by Arthur. Morgan's words were true, and he felt gratitude that someone else recognized it.

"What are you doing in Paris?" Arthur's voice was resigned, as though he chose not to pick this particular battle with his betrothed.

"We had a run in with Malegant."

"In Paris?"

"No, in Champagne. I came through the ley line last night to check on the lead."

"You took Gwin with you?" The protective anger had returned to Arthur's voice. The Lord of Camelot did not countenance any lady being put in harm's way.

"No, she followed me. I didn't know she was there until I was caught. She saved me, but the Champagne manse is destroyed. Malegant and his Templars burned it to the ground."

Lance gave Arthur a moment to let that bit of news sink in. As the solemn silence wafted through the receiver, Lance raised his gaze to find Gwin. Her brows were arched high as they did when something excited her. Had she found something to help in this quest?

No. He couldn't think of it like that. This wasn't a quest, certainly not her quest. He was getting her back to Camelot and the safety of Tintagel as soon as he hung up the phone.

"What's this Malegant after?" asked Morgan.

"He believes that a number of the original Templars were cursed," said Lance. "Turned to stone and sleeping somewhere in France. The man's insane."

"Is that even possible?" Arthur's question wasn't directed at Lance. It was directed at the witch beside him.

"Petrification? It's possible," said Morgan. "No one's figured it out yet that we know of. Well no one mortal, anyway. It's rumored that Rhea had petrified her husband, Cronus."

"The Titans?" asked Lance.

"Yeah," said Morgan. "Vivi told me that that's what Psi told her about his parents. Otherwise, Cronus would be out in this realm crunching on Greeks like pita chips."

"Wait?" said Lance. "Are you saying turning a living person to stone is possible?"

"For gods, yes," said Morgan. "Though I do remember stories of some alchemists in the East working on it. Hey, how's my sister?"

Lance's gaze had never left Gwin. He caught each twist of her lips as she read, each rise of her brow as she turned the page.

"She's fine. She's well. She's unharmed." He fumbled over each of the words. "She was magnificent last night."

Gwin's blue eyes shone bright, as though she'd found something. Lance noted the pregnant pause on the other end of the line. He rushed to fill it.

"In the battle with the Templars, I mean. She probably saved my life."

"You said that already." Arthur's voice was low and controlled. It was a tone Lance also knew well. It told him to tread lightly because the path he was on was dangerous. "Bring her home and we'll meet at the Round Table with the rest of the knights to determine a course of action."

"Or," said Morgan. "They could spend the afternoon in Paris and be home in time for dinner. What's the rush?"

Lance knew the rush, just as well as Arthur. Maybe one day would come a time for he and Gwin to be together. But this was not that day, nor the time.

"We're at Notre Dame," he said. "We'll access the line and be home soon."

18

______

Gwin watched as Lance handed the phone back to the shopkeeper. The woman arched her chest towards him as she took the device. Had two buttons on her blouse come open since they'd come in the store?

Gwin could clearly see the woman's blue, lacy bra. Lady Gwynfhar had taught her daughters that a lady never exposed her undergarments unless she was a lady of the night. It was well after dawn outside the shop.

Lance didn't notice. His gaze remained on Gwin as he passed out of the No Customer zone and came to her. Gwin touched her fingers to the high collar of her blouse. She only just barely resisted the urge to stick out her tongue to the shopkeeper.

"It's time to go home," Lance said when he came to her.

"But I'm not ready." Though she'd stopped herself from sticking out her tongue in a childish move, she did not manage to hold in her sigh of infantile impudence.

Like a parent who'd moved past indulgence, Lance reached out his hand to her and made a come hither motion. Gwin had seen many men do this to their paramours back in Camelot. But Lance wasn't treating her like his lover, at the moment. He was treating her like his wayward charge who was out past her playtime.

"Look at what I found." She held up the book for him, turning it a little to the side so that the ancient script was prominent.

His gaze didn't leave her face at first. But then a second later, he slid his glance towards the words on the page. He shook his head, and then he blinked, leaning in. "My Arabic is a little rusty, but does that say what I think it says?"

Gwin nodded. "What if there is some truth to this Stone Templars notion?"

"We need to get this back home." Lance took the book from her. Placing it under one arm, he looped Gwin under the other and steered them towards the door. Before he could take a step, the store clerk was in front of them.

The unbuttoned woman gave Gwin a stony glare before addressing Lance in clipped English. "You'll need to pay for that book, *monsieur*."

Lance held onto the book and let go of Gwin. He didn't reach into his pockets. Gwin knew he'd already depleted his funds when he'd bought them both clothing. He stepped up to the store clerk, blocking Gwin from the woman's gaze.

"I'm a little low on funds." He spoke in perfect French with a sultry tone. "How about I take your email address and send you the money via an app when I get home?"

The wanton woman grinned as she nodded in agreement. She wrote her email, and phone number, and was that an address? on the back of one of the store's free bookmarks. Lance tucked the bookmark in between the book's pages. He gave the clerk a wink. She leaned in again, the third button of her blouse somehow having come undone. But Lance had already reclaimed Gwin with his free hand and was steering them out of the door.

"Let's get to the church," he said once they were in the warm air.

Gwin stepped closer to him, matching their

strides. She found a Gwin-sized nook in the crook of his shoulder. She wanted to burrow into the spot but didn't.

It was a short stroll to the church. The ancient building swelled with magical energy that the human tourists milling about could likely feel, but would call by another name, like the Holy Spirit. Humans could feel magic, but they couldn't tap into the *spirit* and use it for their liking.

Lance and Gwin entered the church. He allowed Gwin to step in front of him and guide him to the source of the energy where they could open a door and return home. The energy led her to the church sacristy.

With the abundant energy of the ley line, Gwin was able to divert attention away from the room while she called forth the energy to open up a magical pathway. When she was done, she took Lance's hand and they stepped through into the darkness.

His arms came around her in the ether as their molecules were pulled apart and transported across space and time. Gwin couldn't tell where Lance began and she ended. His energy felt as though it had always been a part of her, waiting for a chance to slip past her skin.

He pulled her close. His lips rested in her hair. She only needed to lift her head and she would taste the bristles at his chin.

And so she lifted her head up. She felt his breath as magic swirled around him. They were two puzzle pieces, two sides of a locket that clicked into place. They simply fit.

Once they were deposited at the other end, neither of them reached for the door to let them out on the other side. Their time alone together was almost up or so Lance thought.

"You should know; we're not going home."

His hold didn't loosen. In fact, he pulled her closer, clicking her into the spot in his chest that seemed made for her alone. "Adventure time is over, Gwin. You're going back home where it's safe."

"So that you can go out on your date?"

Lance pulled back to peer down into her face. He stared into her eyes, but she wouldn't meet his gaze. She knew before he even voiced it that he never had any intention of dating the clerk. She also knew he would make good on his promise to pay for the book when they got home.

However, Gwin wasn't going to apologize and let him think she was even more foolish than she already felt. Besides, if she didn't apologize, he'd have to set her straight on her misperception and Gwin ached to be reassured of his feelings for her.

"You know better," he said.

She nodded, finally looking up. Clear blue eyes shone down on her with the light of truth. His feelings for her were undeniable.

"There's only one woman my heart has ever belonged to. Only one woman that has ever held my attention."

A stray bit of air from the other side of the door blew in through the cracks. The breeze blew across her face, pulling strands of her hair loose from the haphazard braid she'd made of her locks. Lance's fingers hesitated, but in the end, he brushed the hair from her cheek escorting it across the bridge of her nose, over her lower eyelid, until it was back where it belonged behind her ear.

"I'm not interested in that woman's email address or her phone number," he said. "I've only ever wanted to call you. I've only ever wanted to email you."

His lips closed and then parted, but no words came out. He looked up, a shadow of guilt darkening his face as the sun moved higher in the sky. A trace remained when his gaze found hers again. His voice was a hushed whisper as he spoke.

"It looks like I may be able to make that call in the future."

Now it was Gwin's turn to open her mouth without any words escaping. Her heart filled her chest, like a balloon expanding to capacity. She was certain that with just the tiniest inhale she'd burst.

"You'll be free soon," he continued.

She wanted to tell him that she was free now. That she'd never been touched. But the bells of the church rang, startling them both out of the magical moment.

She didn't feel the pressure to reach out and grab it back to her. He was right. They could be together soon. Regardless of whether Merlin stayed on this plane of existence or his soul soon went back to his maker, Gwin was determined to start her life with Lance sooner rather than later.

"We can wait," he said. "For now, let's get you inside."

He twined his fingers with hers. He gave a tug, but she didn't move. She was willing to wait to be with him. She was not willing to let this adventure end just yet.

"Gwin?"

"We're not home. We're in Arville."

"Arville?"

"It was one of the last preceptories of the Templar Knights. The text mentions that de Molay spent time here. It's where he was ordained. It's very likely that they'll have records of his life that aren't in these books."

"That would mean it's a Templar stronghold." Lance's hold on her tightened, and he reached for the brooch she knew was his sword.

"It was purchased from the Templars centuries ago and is run by the state."

"Gwin, you're not going to Arville."

"We're already here."

Lance looked up at the closed door, as though finally realizing the meaning of her words. "My lady, you are not going out there." He gave her a tug.

"Good sir, I am, too." Gwin would not budge.

His blue eyes darkened. She watched the wheels turn over in his head as he weighed his options. "I'll throw you over my shoulder," he said.

She lifted an eyebrow, daring him. He pursed his lips. It was kind of adorable and not to mention empowering. Polite, obedient Lady Gwin had strong-armed the fiercest knight of the Round Table.

"Just one hour," she said. "I won't leave your sight. I'll stick to the books. And at any sign of danger, of which I doubt there'll be any, I'll head back to the ley line."

Lance's muscles remained rock hard with tension. His brow pinched. A tick clicked rhythmically in his jaw.

"Just this one last adventure," she said. "And then I'll go home and be a proper young miss again who won't give you any trouble. I promise."

She felt his indecision. It looked as though she were wearing him down. She would never know.

The door opened. There wasn't much light on the other side. Still, the glint of multiple swords was clear to see in the dark, dank room.

Gwin dropped de Molay's journal to the stone floor. The ancient tome made a sickening thud that Gwin knew was the cracking of the manuscript's spine. She had no time to mourn the damage of the book. She put her hands into the air.

19

It was like being awakened from a wet dream and tossed into boiling water. One moment, Lance had Gwin in his arms, her lips so close to his. That was the dream he had every night, an almost kiss because even in his secret dreams he wouldn't cross the line of impropriety. There had never been a sword in his dream.

The business end of a blade wasn't just pointing at his gut. No, that was a normal dream for him. A night terror, that was par for the course for men of action. Hell, it was a normal Tuesday for him to be on the receiving end of a weapon in his wakefulness. But never her.

There was a blade pointing at Gwin's breasts. No. This would not do. But what could he do?

His first instinct was to go through the sword at his gut to get to the one at her breast. That maneuver would leave her alone and at the mercy of Malegant's villains. As inept as they were, they could still do damage in numbers.

He could shove her behind him and take both mortal points. His death would give her time to reopen the ley line and get to safety. Yes, that was the only solution.

It wasn't his own life Lance cared for. It was only hers. Always her. But how to get her to agree?

"You promised that if there was danger," he began, "you would turn around."

"I lied," said Gwin. She bristled at his side. The defiance rolled off her like a cold breeze from the north on a summer's day.

"You have always been a lady of your word," Lance said. "I need you to keep your word now."

"I won't leave you to die. If you die, I come with you."

How could his fondest wish and night terror occupy the same space? Lance felt no joy in her words. Determination rose in his chest and steeled his spine. Whatever happened, she would live.

Lance peered into the darkness, trying to find an advantage, or at least determine how many attackers they faced. There wasn't much to see except black and shadows. On the positive side, they hadn't been struck through yet, so there was a chance.

All Lance saw were the hands that held the swords. One left, one right. One attacker? The fingers of both hands were gnarled. The skin wrinkled, as though the warrior who held the swords was old. And then the sword aimed at Gwin lowered.

"Forgive me, my lady," came a hollow, creaky voice. "I did not see that there was a noble creature in my presence. My apologies for raising my blade."

As though by magic, a spark of illumination lit the room. Standing before them was the thinnest bear of a man Lance had ever seen. Long, white strands of hair fell from the man's cheeks and chin all the way down to his chest. The same puffy hair covered his head. He wore a dingy white tunic that had seen better days. On his chest, there was a crimson red cross. Not the straight-lined cross that was the mark of Christ. The tops of each point of the cross on the man's chest were triangular. It was the original mark of the Order of Solomon, the original Templars.

Was it possible? Was this a Templar of Solomon? If so, why was the blade still trained on Lance?

The old man bowed his head in deference to

Gwin. The blade he held at Lance's gut never wavered, never wobbled like Malegant's Templars who were all barely a quarter of this man's age.

"Thank you, kind sir," said Gwin. "Now would you mind lowering your blade on my companion?"

"I'm an observant man in my old age. I notice you, my lady, wear a wedding band where your *companion* does not. I notice you call him *companion* instead of husband. I know no knight of honor would dare dally with a lady, especially a witch, that was not his wife."

That called Lance up short. Already, the familiar feeling of heat spread through his body. Not a heat of desire, a feverish heat that left him feeling ill to his stomach. A sickness that wracked his person. A debilitating malady that had never been within his control.

"If he were a knight of Camelot, he would abide by the code of chivalry," said the Templar.

The blade at Lance's gut ceased to be a dilemma. He unclenched his fists and let his hands hang at his side. He was defenseless against these accusations.

For one hundred years, he'd lived by the code, determined to prove himself worthy of honor and eschew the caste his father's actions had bred him in. If Lance were honest, he'd acknowledge he'd danced on the edges of the code when it came to Gwin. There had never been any physical impropriety before today. But for decades, there had been infidelity in his heart, in his mind, in his soul.

"Sir Lancelot is all that is honorable and good. He's the best man I know." Gwin stepped in front of Lance, inserting herself between Lance's gut and the Templar's blade. "I'm nearly widowed, and I intend to make him my husband very soon. So, good sir, if you intend to take his life, you'll take mine as well."

The Templar's sword lowered at Gwin's good word. However, Lance saw in the Templar's eyes that the man's estimation of him hadn't raised an inch.

The old man sheathed both swords, and then turned to Gwin, offering his arm. "Nearly widowed?"

Lance felt the sigh of relief sail through Gwin's body as she took the proffered arm. "It's a long story. My name is Gwin."

"I know who you are, my dear. I may live a world away from Camelot, but I know its tales well. I am Sir Bernard Darvill, at your service."

"You're of the original Order of Templars?"

Though Sir Darvill had held his swords like a man of twenty, his body moved like a man past his prime. His back hunched now that the danger was over. His knees creaked as he moved.

"I'm likely the last of my kind," the old man said. "I can trace my line back six hundred years. I'm 105 just this past year."

"Wouldn't have pegged you for a day over ninety," Lance muttered.

The knight glared. Nothing wrong with his hearing apparently.

"The order had dwindled to only a few families during the time of my grandfather. My brothers didn't choose the life. Unfortunately, I had no sons. So, the line ends with me."

"My grandfather, Sir Galahad, only had daughters," said Gwin. "No sons. His two daughters kept the name. The line of heritage has done quite nicely with the three Galahad girls that remain."

"Daughters would've been lovely, but I had no children. I had no wife." He paused, looking off into the distance out of a stained glass window. They'd come up a creaking stairwell into what looked like an abandoned church.

Lance knew the look Sir Darvill wore. The old knight may not have had a wife, but he had loved once. Likely from afar if the crinkle at his eye was a clue.

"I had loved," Darvill confirmed. "I chose my duty over her."

Gwin looked down to the flooring as they made their way through the pews. She didn't turn to look at Lance, who trailed behind Gwin and Darvill. She didn't need to. They were seeing their future play out in the sad eyes of the old knight.

"I watched her move on with her life, marry and have children, then grow old and lay to rest. I watched over her her entire life, loving her from afar as I kept my vows. It was enough."

That last line was spoken with a hint of bitterness coating the longing. Lance saw a flicker of regret in the old man's eyes. It was the same flicker he confronted in the mirror each day.

It was a lie. What Sir Darvill had traded, love for duty, it wasn't enough. Lance wouldn't call the man on his broken vow of honesty. He was more interested in not repeating the man's lifelong mistake.

"It's been a long time since a witch or one of Arthur's knights has graced this place," said Sir Darvill, his voice perking up. "Tell me, what brings you two here to the Commandery of Arville?"

20

They left the church and moved across the grounds. Behind the property was farmland, but woods bordered the fertile ground. Gwin knew from her quick research into the Arville Perceptory that the stone church was built in the twelfth century. There were three semicircular archways that symbolized the Holy Trinity.

To the right of the church was a Tithe Barn. The doors to the barn were open. However, it was clear to see the innards were empty. As too was the actual barn that should've housed livestock.

"Are there others?" asked Gwin.

"It is only I," said Sir Darvill. "I am the last of my kind. No boy band. Just a solo act."

Sir Darvill turned and sneered at Lance. Before the elderly knight turned back to face Gwin, Gwin saw Lance raise his arms as though to say *What did I do to you*? Lance's gaze fell to where Gwin's arm rested in the crook of the Templar's elbow.

Gwin chuckled, giving Lance an affectionate smile. She'd seen his face fall when Sir Darvill had attacked his honor. That was a wound that cut deeper than a sword.

Lance had pulled his mask of nonchalance over his features. It was his Hostess Smile. The two of them had that in common, always hiding what they truly wanted. Well, that would end soon.

Actually, no. It had already ended. Yesterday was the last day that she would ever deny or suppress her feelings for this man. From this and every day forward, she'd live in the light of truth. That truth was that she loved Lancelot and had every intention of being his bride, his wife, his partner for life.

With that knowledge, Gwin practically skipped along as Sir Darvill led her to the commandery's central holding; the preceptory. A preceptory was the headquarters of any knights' property. Gwin hadn't been to many outside of those that belonged to Camelot. It was too dangerous to go to old monastic commanderies because it was unclear if it was now a Templar stronghold. The building they walked into was dubbed The Center for Chivalric Orders, but Gwin knew it was originally a stable.

In its heyday, the commandery would be used mainly for farming, religious life, and military training for knights awaiting deployment to the Crusades. History told this place had fallen to the Hospitallers of Saint John of Jerusalem. The turrets were a Hospitaller addition. Gwin knew so because she could tell the pinnacles were covered with chestnut tiles, better known as shingles. The tithe barn was also made of chestnut. Only the chapel told of its ancient connection to Camelot. It was built with stone, as Camelot built its castles and strongholds.

"The history records told that this place was bought by Hospitallers after the Templar Order was abolished," she said.

"We had to hide what we truly were for a time," said Sir Darvill. "My ancestors called themselves Hospitallers, but we never abandoned what we truly were. After the Friday the 13th Massacre, and later the French Revolution, we kept a low profile. My grandfather had the idea to turn the land into a tourist attraction to hide in plain sight. It's evident we don't get many venturing out here to see the dregs of an ancient way of life that has nearly died out."

The true allegiance of this place was most evident in the preceptory's Great Hall. On the wall hung the vows of the Templars. Today's Templars followed ten pillars of Chivalry. The original Templars followed twelve. The first two of the twelve read:

Preserve the ancient origins of religion and spirituality.
Seek communion with the feminine face of God.

*I*f she had any more doubt, all of her defenses relaxed now. Sir Bernard Darvill was a friend of Camelot. A witch would know no harm in his care. She only wished she'd known he was out here sooner. She would insisted he come back with them to Camelot and be amongst his own kind because the original Templars were protectors of magical kind just like their brothers, the Knights of Camelot.

"Now, how can I be of assistance to you, my lady?"

"We're looking for records of Jacques de Molay's time in the East." She decided not to go into the reasons why. Though Gwin had lived her entire life in a world of the fantastical, she knew that the idea of men turned to stone was a bit out there.

"De Molay spent a lot of time here," said Darvill. "Much of his writing is stored here."

Darvill led them into a room that looked like an ancient library. That wasn't their final destination. He pressed a stone and a doorway opened revealing a secret passageway. Fluorescent stones lined the walls and ceilings shedding colorful light. Inside the room were rows upon rows of ancient binders. Gwin knew her cousin, Loren, and her bestie, Nia, would expire on the spot over the sight of the tomes.

"You'll find de Molay's journals over there," said Sir Darvill. "I'll prepare luncheon and leave you to it."

"We won't be staying that long," said Lance.

Darvill glared at him as he made his way to the door. "In my days, knights were hospitable. They always offered sustenance to their guests, especially if that guest was a lady."

Lance grit his teeth, obviously reaching for

patience. "You'll understand, sir, that I need to return the lady to the safety of Tintagel Castle."

"Are you saying this fortress isn't safe, *sir*?"

Lance's mouth opened and closed. He was caught between a rock and a hard place. Gwin decided to step in and soften the blow.

"We would love a repast before we journey home," said Gwin. "You're too kind, Sir Darvill."

Sir Darvill turned to beam at her. He gave her a deep bow that she worried he wouldn't rise from. He managed to rise, but not before he glared at Lance and then turned to leave.

"What did I do to him?" grumbled Lance.

"You're used to being perfect," Gwin said as she took a seat and opened the first book.

"No one thinks I'm perfect," said Lance. "I'm a bastard, remember."

"No." Gwin's fingers paused in turning the page. They had to get this straight right now. "You are not a bastard. You were born out of wedlock. That is not a smear on your character. It's not even a smear on your mother's character because she loved and trusted your father. The only person whose reputation should be tarnished is the former Sir Lancelot, who I hope is being tormented in hell for what he put both you, your mother, and his wife through."

A tentative smile started at the corner of his mouth. His voice was soft and halting when he spoke. "I don't think I've ever heard you speak so uncharitably about another living soul."

"Life is a miracle and precious. Your life is precious to me. I don't care how you got here, only that you are here."

He brushed a hand over his face, likely trying to hide his emotions from her. She'd allow him this one last time. But this was it.

She would not spend her life in an old crypt, aging and alone. She would reach for the one she loved and hold him near for the rest of her days. But first, she had a mission to complete.

Gwin put her head into the book as Lance milled about the room. He couldn't seem to keep still, vacillating between watching the door, watching her, and playing with the brooch that contained his sword.

Jacques de Molay had kept meticulous notes of his time as Grand Master. The journal Gwin found first was the last journal he'd written. In it, she learned of the struggles of the last days of the Templars. De Molay wasn't only contending with his enemies of the crown and in the church, he also fought off other orders.

De Molay had allies in Cyprus, Persia, Spain, and

even England. As the French King and Pope began to tighten the noose around the Templars' necks, these other powers offered protection, if the Templars merged with their orders.

Orders from as far away as England. It would appear that the English King, Edward I, pressed the hardest. But de Molay maintained the Templar's autonomy. He vowed the order would not be folded into another's military. He wrote that he suspected there were traitors inside the order, angling to align the knights with the Papacy. The last entry was of de Molay contemplating a parlay that would take him to England. He wrote of a request to meet at Carnac with the king's knights.

"I think I've found something." Lance had stopped his pacing and was bent over a book.

Gwin went to him. Looking at the date of the writings, these were from de Molay's early times as an ordained knight.

"This is from his time in Persia with the Mongols of the Ilkhanate," he said. "There's a ley line there, isn't there?"

There was a ley line there, and a small community of magical kind. Gwin had never visited herself, but some of the wizards there had made the journey to Camelot a few times in her life. Morgan was always thrilled at their arrival. They were of the few magical kind who still practiced alchemy.

Gwin turned a few pages of the journal, and there it was. By the tiny intake of breath at her ear, Lance saw it too. Beside notes about petrification written in French, was a scrawled bit of Arabic. The same bit of Arabic a bystander had reported that de Molay had shouted on the day of his death by fire and drowning on a stake overlooking the Seine.

Gwin's written Arabic was rusty. The language was often spoken back at home, but few wrote it. She sounded the words out, her voice quiet in the cavernous room.

"Taslib alqalb waljism lilhimaya." It roughly translated to *harden the heart and body for protection.*

She heard Lance gasp. But it was louder than a gasp. The intake of breath wasn't one of surprise. It was one of pain.

Gwin looked up to find Lance gripping his heart. His eyes went large. He opened his mouth to speak, but nothing came out. His hand went for his sword but his fingers wouldn't uncurl.

Gwin reached for him, her heart in her throat to see him in pain. When she touched him, his skin was rough, like tree bark. Under her fingertips, his flesh was smoothing out and getting colder, like stone.

He was being petrified before her eyes. It was the words. It was the spell. Lance was turning to stone.

21

———

*L*ance had been too busy watching Gwin's lips as they whispered the spell to notice that the words were having an effect on him. Whenever she spoke, the words always arrowed straight to his heart. These words were no different. But instead of warming his heart, everything went cold.

"Lance? Lance!"

Gwin's words fell away. The sound of his name moving farther and farther away from him even though she stood right in front of him. She reached out to him, running her fingers over his face, his chest. The cruel reality was that he felt none of her touch.

He was trapped in a nightmare. Unable to close

his eyes as the real world continued to turn around him. He couldn't move. He couldn't speak. He could barely think.

It felt like the phenomenon known as having a witch on your back. That paralysis that came with sleep that felt as though an old hag sat on your back or on your chest.

The witch in front of Lance was lovely with flawless skin that was coloring a panicked shade of red. Her bright eyes glistened with fear. Her kissable lips were stretched taut as she yelled words that he couldn't respond to.

That's when he started to panic. Gwin was in jeopardy. He had to save her. Had to protect her. But he couldn't move his hand to raise his sword. He couldn't lift his foot to place himself in front of her.

He was shaking, though his limbs were rigid. His heart raced, about to explode in the confined container of its prison. His gut, his head, all were rock hard and impenetrable. He couldn't reach out to her.

Lance had always thought he'd die by the sword. Or, if he was lucky, dragon's fire while retrieving a treasure of Camelot. Maybe a raging demigod might break his spine after Lance successfully protected his city and his people. But this, this impotency to protect his lady, this was a fate worse than death.

And then, just as suddenly as he'd been rendered stiff and immobile, he was free.

Gwin's healing hands were around him. She held him tight, brushing away the crust of gravel that had imprisoned him. Her heat suffused him, returning life to his limbs and his soul.

Lance threw propriety out of the window. He brought his hands around her. He lifted her light form onto his lap, locked his arms around her, and buried his face in her neck.

"I'm so sorry," she said. "I'm so sorry."

Gwin repeated the words on a loop. She ran her fingers through his hair, digging her nails into his scalp. With her other hand, she pressed her palm into his back, pulling him closer into her embrace.

"The curse is real." Lance's voice creaked like a twig breaking in half on a hot day.

He pulled Gwin even tighter to him, fitting her head in the crook of his neck until he felt her hot breath on his skin. The pulsing life of her was necessary after his brief foray into the dark stillness of that curse. He felt it clawing at his skin, still resting on the fine hairs on his forearms waiting to wrap him up again.

"There may be hundreds, thousands of men who were petrified hundreds of years ago," she said. "We have to find them."

Lance pulled away, just a few inches. Only far enough so that he could peer down into her face. "No, we don't."

Lance had not a care of finding Templars turned to stone. His mission remained the same, and he would not be deterred any longer. He was getting her back behind the impenetrable walls of Tintagel Castle. This adventure was over.

Gwin tilted her head back and frowned at him. For a second, Lance forgot that they were arguing. She looked lovely, adorable, kissable. It took his body turning to stone to release any more doubts, any more blocks. Gwin belonged in his arms.

"You endured that suffering for only a few moments," she said. "Those men have endured it for centuries."

"Which means they're likely dead." And good riddance. It meant the knights wouldn't have to find somewhere to house a few hundred of their foes.

"Not if they were magical kind." She sat up on his lap, her arms looped around his neck. "In fact, I don't think the spell would have worked unless they were magical kind. There'd have to be parameters on it. Why those two words; heart and stone?"

Her gaze trailed off as she turned the words over in her head. Lance watched her for a moment. He marveled that their position was so comfortable; her sitting on his lap in a loose embrace as they conversed. It was as though they'd been lovers for decades.

The truth is they had. They'd just never had occasion to touch in this manner.

Gwin traced her fingers through his hair again and again as she gazed off into the distance, lost in thought. Lance might be ready for their adventure to be over. But he was now more than ready for their love story to begin in earnest.

He leaned into her touch, feeling whole for the first time in his life. He'd felt her fingertips on him before. But she wasn't trying to heal him now. Right now, she only wanted to touch him.

Lance tilted his head up to see her face. Her gaze was focused on the strands of his hair slipping between her fingers. They'd spent so much time in close proximity but so far apart from each other.

He thought back to the last time he was this close to her, the day they'd met. The day his life changed forever because he'd fallen so deeply, so completely in love with her.

She turned back to him, focusing on the present instead of the past. He focused on her lips, waiting for words to form. None did. Neither of them had any protest left in them. They both knew this was inevitable. So why not right now?

But Gwin didn't take the last inch that would bring her to his hungry mouth. Somehow, his desire-addled brain remembered why. She said she wouldn't be the one to make this move again. It was up to him.

Lance rushed head first into this battle and won. He slanted his lips over Gwin's. It was not a tentative kiss. It was not a seeking kiss. It was a kiss of victory, a kiss of ownership. This was a battle he'd won long ago, and now, finally, he took possession of his prize.

Lance plundered Gwin's mouth, and she let him in. Her lips parted like a drawbridge opening for the onslaught. Because it was an onslaught.

Lance was so desperate for her that he nicked the top of her plump lips. He'd drawn first blood. Instead of stopping and pulling away to tend the wound, he sucked at her injury and pushed deeper. There was nothing and no one that would keep them apart any longer.

The sound of a clearing throat didn't tear him away from her. It was the shove against his shoulder that did.

Lance looked up to see Sir Darvill glaring down at him as though he were the rat the cat dragged in. The look almost colored Lance's vision to a guilty shade of gray. But the shade of remorse refused to fall.

Lance held the woman he loved in his arms. The woman who loved him back. The woman that would soon, one day, after her husband died, of course, and then there would be a short period of mourning, and likely a period of courtship where he made his intentions plain, after all that, then she would wholly and completely be his.

"Sorry to interrupt your *tête-á-tête*," said the knight without any remorse. "I thought I was having a heart attack or a stroke a moment ago when I was rendered immobile."

"I'm so sorry, Sir Darvill," said Gwin, coming to stand before the elder knight. Her hands already warming with her healing magic as she looked for a place to soothe his old bones. "That was my fault. I found a spell and—"

"I figured it was a spell," said Darvill, smiling kindly down upon her. "When a witch turns up looking for de Molay's journals, I assumed you were searching for any evidence of the Stone Templars myth."

"So it is true?" Gwin breathed.

Darvill shrugged. "I don't know for sure. Only tales. But we have a bigger problem heading our way. When I came too, I saw a caravan coming down the road. Newer cars, military style. No one in the village drives anything fancier than a pickup truck."

Lance looked to Gwin. They both knew who had that style of cars. Malegant and his men.

22

Dust and gravel kicked up behind the two jeeps headed down the unpaved road toward the commandery. Magic itched in the center of Gwin's palms at the approach of Malegant and his goons. Memories of what they'd done churned inside her gut. The feeling was instantly cooled as Lance laced his fingers with hers.

With his other hand, Lance freed his sword from its adorned hiding place. He turned to Darvill. "Is there any other way out of here?"

"You want to run?" Sir Darvill's tone was indignant. "I'll stand and face my adversaries."

"And put a witch's life in danger? She is our priority."

That brought the elderly knight up short.

Already, Malegant's men had parked in front of the church and were filing out of their vehicles. Darvill looked left and right, just as Gwin had already done. She had to guess the older knight came away with the same conclusion. If the three of them tried to make a run for the church and the ley line, they would be spotted. Gwin might not be able to cast the spell quick enough to outrun their guns.

"There is a passageway beneath the Hall," Darvill said to Lance. "It leads to the church. We'll need to provide a distraction so that she can get out."

"I'm not leaving without you," Gwin said to Lance. She pressed her palm to his. With her free hand, she wound it around his bicep like a vise. "We run or stay together."

Lance's eyes searched hers. Only a moment ago, the two of them had been locked in a passionate embrace. She'd been pliant in his hold, had yielded to every flick of his tongue, to his every nibble at her lip, to his groan demanding more of her. Gwin would not budge now. She knew he saw it in her eyes when he turned to Sir Darvill and motioned for the old man to precede them to the secret passageway.

Lance's hold on Gwin was iron-clad as they stole through the halls of the commandery. This place was a fortress. During its heyday, it would've been impenetrable by a cannon that could fire once or twice in an hour. But with modern-day armed forces, it would not hold for long. The inhabitants inside would soon turn into sitting ducks only good for target practice.

The three went down into a lower level. The air got thinner, damper. But the magic got stronger. They were near the church.

As they inched closer, the air thickened. The dark wetness dried up. Warmth flooded the small space. Not in a way that simply warmed the skin. Gwin began to feel like she was a pig on a roast.

"They've set the church on fire," said Darvill.

They came to a dead halt. They couldn't move forward. The ceiling of the cavern was the floor of the church. Already the stone walls were too hot to touch.

Lance scooped Gwin into his arms. Before he could take too many steps she squirmed in his hold.

"No," she insisted. "Help Sir Darvill."

Conflict was fleeting on Lance's face. He set Gwin down and turned to give his shoulder to the slower moving Darvill. The desire for life won out against pride in the old man and the two knights moved quickly through the caverns together with Gwin in the lead.

Coming out the other end, they were at the back of the hall. But they weren't alone. Gwin heard voices coming toward them down the hall.

Peering out the door, she saw that they were pushed up against the forest wall. She opened the door and stepped out into the cool air. She didn't get far before Lance wrapped his arms around her and pulled her back inside.

"Where do you think you're going?" he demanded.

"We can make a run for the tree line and hide until they're gone."

Lance shook his head. Darvill came over his shoulder, his face set in a grim line that backed up Lance's stance on the matter.

"It was fine to run to get you to safety," said Lance. "Now that we're cornered, we will stand and fight. It's the only honorable thing to do."

"I stand at the ready to fight by your side sir," said Sir Darvill. "And if today be the day I go to my glory, it has been my honor to be in your service, Lady Gwin."

The two were mad. They had a plausible getaway before them. But their egos got in their way and they preferred to rush into danger. For what? For honor!

Darvill pulled this sword. The steel glinted and hummed. With all the magic running underfoot, Gwin hadn't realized that Darvill's sword was made of the same magical ore as the swords of Camelot. He had both the blood of a knight and the metal.

Heart and stone.

Before Lance had kissed her and he'd been only holding her in his arms for comfort, Gwin had been thinking. She'd been trying to understand how that spell had worked on him? She hadn't aimed it at him, she'd only said the words.

Most spells had to have a direction, an intention. She'd had no intention when she'd said the words aloud. But they went straight for him. And for Sir Darvill, who'd been some distance away.

There was magic in the swords. There was also magic in the men. Could it be that the words of de Molay's spell had woven together to affect anyone who held those two requirements?

It was magic, unlike anything Gwin had ever witnessed. Magic she didn't even know was possible. It was magic that went against someone's will; a curse. Gwin had never uttered a curse in her life.

Both men brandished their swords, preparing to

rush into a battle that would definitely be the end of Sir Darvill, and at best, would maim Lance.

God, sometimes she really hated the tenets of chivalry. That code would be the death of these men. It had been the death of many good men in the past.

Why wouldn't they just run from the danger? Perhaps if she got them to stand still until the danger passed ...

Gwin spoke the words she didn't think she would ever speak again. She didn't see any other choice. The curse instantly shushed their bravado.

Lance's tan arms turned peat brown, then dull gray. The soft place where he'd held her turned hard. The last thing she saw was the spark of anger in Lance's eyes before his body was encased in stone.

For a moment, Gwin panicked, thinking she'd killed him. But her own heart still beat. That's how she knew he lived. She still felt his energy and Darvill's.

They were alive. They looked like two boulders set apart from the forest. Hidden from the eyes of others.

Could there be other men encased in this way? Hundreds of men. For hundreds of years. The poor souls. She had to find them.

She couldn't focus on that now. The Templars of

today were entering the building. Gwin had been able to hide the knights. Because she had no sword, she was now the only sitting duck.

She needed to duck inside the passageway. She took a step, but a figure moved into view. Gwin slipped behind the Lance-boulder, pressing her warm back to his stony face.

"I'm getting tired of this guy," came one of the voices of the Templars. He had an Eastern European accent. "We've been driving around for days, and we haven't seen one of these stone men. I'm starting to think he's full of shit."

"We did see that witch," said the other man.

The two men stood near the Darvill-stone. Gwin held her breath as the men continued to moan their grievances of knighthood.

"Did we really? All we saw were books flying through the air. It could've been rigged. And where are these riches Malegant keeps talking about? Have you seen any gold or gems or treasure?"

"What are you gonna do? Go back to your day job?"

He kicked at the Darvill stone. "I don't know, man? But I'm starting to think I'm wasting my time out here."

"You two," yelled a booming voice.

Gwin peered from behind the protection of the stone-faced Lance. She recognized the Templar as the brute from back in Champagne, the one who'd held the blade to Lance's neck.

"You find anyone out here?" the Brute called.

"No," said the Doubter. "Just us and some rocks."

"Whoever was here, they took off," said the Brute. "Most likely through the church. There's a ley line in there. So, we torched it."

"Great," muttered The Doubter. "Signed on to be a knight and I'm reduced to an arsonist."

"What was that?" growled The Brute.

"Nothing," The Doubter said more clearly.

In the tense silence that followed, Gwin imagined a stare-off between the two. She doubted the naysayer would come out victorious.

"There's nothing here," said the Brute.

Good. They hadn't found the secret library.

"The Stone Templars didn't make it this far south," said the Brute, breaking the tense silence. "Malegant found some kind of book. He thinks they were closer to Paris or closer to the north near the border. We're taking off."

The men made their way across the path. Gwin still didn't move until she heard the squeal of wheels tear out. Finally, she let out the breath she'd been holding. As the fire blazed from the church, she pulled magic from the ley energy and cast another spell.

Lance fell into her arms, limbs shivering, his eyes burning bright. "Don't you ever dare do that again!"

23

Lance fought through the stiffness and cold and reached for Gwin. Unlike his touches earlier where he brought her to him for a caress, or when he'd wrapped her in the protection of his embrace, he dug his fingers into her shoulders and gave her a shake.

Her blue eyes widened. The light of love blinked out. When her eyes opened again, there was a tinge of fear.

Good. He needed her to be afraid. He'd been terrified when he'd been encased in stone. He'd been petrified, literally. Those men had come so near her, and he couldn't move. If they had harmed her ...

Lance pulled Gwin to him, crushing her body to

his. He felt the quickening of her pulse, the pounding of her heart, the gush of her breath.

"Don't ever do that again." His voice was a desperate plea whispered into her ear.

"I only wanted to protect you, to keep you safe."

"I gave my solemn vow that I would protect you with my life," he said. "You had no right to take that from me."

He pulled away, expecting an argument. Instead, her arms came around his neck and held. All of his fear and anger left his system under the touch of her warm hands.

"Lance? Am I not your equal?"

The double negative threw him. His reflexes were still lax having been bound in stone. He was also distracted by the rush of Gwin's sweet scent surrounding him.

"Yes?" he said.

That must've been the right answer because she smiled at him. Danger signs blared somewhere in his mind. He registered the warning as a puissant gnat as this butterfly batted her wings at him.

"I'm not fragile, or helpless, or a victim. I never have been, despite the choices I've made in my life. We're not starting this relationship with me cast as some distressed damsel and you the dashing hero.

Chivalry dies today. It's done nothing but ruin our lives."

Lance exhaled. He felt three centuries old all of a sudden. Likely because he hadn't slept a wink in the last twenty-four hours and he'd been running on adrenalin with mishap after disaster.

He knew Gwin was strong and brave and capable. She was a Galahad girl. But she had a point.

Their vows had kept them apart and miserable for decades. Was that the endgame of chivalry? Misery.

They were each the most devout individuals in their town. They were also the most unhappy. That would change. But not right at this moment.

"I'll vow anything you want," he said. "Once I get you home."

"Deal."

"We need to get out of here," said Lance. "They may come back. Sir Darvill grab only what's necessary and let's go."

Darvill, who'd remained quiet during their whole intimate exchange, shook his head. "I'm not going anywhere. I will not leave my post."

Beside him, Lance felt Gwin sigh. The man was proving her point. Darvill had nothing left and still, he would remain.

"You could have a new beginning, a new life, filled with others, like you," said Gwin "It's not too late for you."

"You're right, my lady." Darvill looked toward the horizon. "I may take a second look at the choices I've made in my life. Who knows? Perhaps my equal is somewhere beyond this fortress."

"So, you'll come with us?"

"Not until I see to the last of my duties."

They all looked over at the burning church.

"At least let us help you put out the fire from the church," said Lance.

"No," said Darvill. "Let it burn. The flames can be seen from miles. If it stops they'll come back. Besides, we all know that God lives in the hearts and not in a building."

"But you'll be cut off from us," said Gwin.

"With all due respect, my lady, I've been cut off all my life. I'm glad you came to visit. You are welcome back any time. I'll never be too far from this place. It's still my duty. But it will no longer be my life."

"How are we going to get out of here?" asked Lance.

Darvill pulled keys from his pocket. "Take my

truck. It's parked on the other side of the forest. There's a path through that cluster of trees there."

The men clasped forearms. Gwin planted a chaste kiss on Darvill's cheek. Then she and Lance went through the cluster of trees.

Gwin and Lance were silent on their trek through the forest. They came out the other end to a beat up truck that looked as old as Darvill.

Lance opened the passenger door and helped Gwin in. He rounded the truck and climbed behind the wheel. It took a few tries before the jalopy turned over and they were off.

They drove through the scenic French countryside in silence. He took the long road that would lead them back to Paris and back to the Notre Dame ley line. He wanted to be careful to avoid Malegant and his men. It would take four hours, but that's only if he did the speed limit. Lance pushed the ancient truck to its limit on the deserted road.

Gwin sat close to the passenger-side door, leaning against the windowsill watching the sun as it began its descent down below the horizon.

"I'm sorry for being rough with you earlier," he said.

She said nothing, but he knew she'd heard him.

"That's my nightmare. Seeing you in danger and being unable to save you."

She turned to him and placed her hand on his knee. Her heated touch warmed him instantly. She wasn't using magic. She simply *was* magic.

Lance's foot let up off the gas a bit. The scenery stopped being a blur. He made out the details of flowers on the side of the road.

"I'm fine," she said. "I'm here with you. Exactly where I belong. Exactly where I want to be."

"I need to get you home, to safety."

"I'll go. I'll do as you wish."

Lance blinked and let out a laugh. "I don't think those words have ever been uttered by a Galahad girl in the history of the world."

Gwin grinned. One of his hands came off the steering wheel and met hers. Their fingers intertwined.

"When we get home," she said, "we're going to talk about our future. Because, Lance, we deserve a future together."

He nodded as they continued toward the horizon. Finally, things were going his way. That's when the truck grumbled, sputtered, and came to a halt.

24

The sun had tucked itself beneath the horizon thirty minutes ago. They all stood at the side of the road under the cover of darkness; Gwin, Lance, and the truck which had come to an abrupt halt. She and Lance had no flashlight and didn't dare use the flares. Instead, Gwin held her palms under the hood. Her witch fire illuminated the engine, and the man bent under the hood.

Gwin couldn't help but admire Lance's backside. It was round and firm. Not too high, like a woman's rear. Not too full, like someone with extra baggage.

Lance had always filled out his pants nicely. His shirts too. Now she had the occasion to look her fill instead of stealing furtive glances.

"Gwin, can you raise the light?"

Her hands had sunk down lower to get a closer, brighter look at the junk under his trunk instead of the hood. She raised her hands. But not her gaze.

Lance bent farther under the hood. The move lifted the right cheek of his backside. Gwin bit her lip, wondering if she'd get the chance to bite that part of skin.

It wasn't that she'd had no occasion to see a naked man or his rear. She'd seen enough of Merlin. His skin was pasty and pale. His body thin and flabby at the same time. Merlin's ass was flat and jiggled as he'd turn in his bed. Not their bed. Merlin was often in a sick bed which left Gwin sleeping elsewhere in their quarters.

That would no longer be her life. She and Lance would share the same bed. He'd roll around in the covers with her. She'd grab his firm ass and—

"Gwin?"

She snapped back to the present. Her hands hadn't fallen down. They were glowing brightly. She gave her wrists a shake and then her whole body.

"Are you cold?" Lance asked.

"No. I'm quite warm, actually."

Satisfied of her well-being, Lance turned back to his frustrations beneath the hood of the truck.

"Come on, you ancient piece of scrap, or I'll put

you in neutral and push you to a junkyard," he growled.

Gwin couldn't hide her grin. She knew the knights preferred fast German and Italian cars when they weren't riding magical horses.

Lance lifted from beneath the hood. He swiped a hand over his forehead and smeared oil on his brow. Gwin giggled and then reached out for him. She wiped her hand over his face. The heat of her magic rubbed the stain off his face.

"Thank you." The frustration had burned from his face along with the slick of oil.

"You're welcome."

In the quiet of the night, Gwin heard the sound of twin thumps. One after the other. The thumping increased in speed and resonance until the sounds became one. Her heartbeat was now in sync with Lance's.

She flicked out her tongue to moisten her lower lip. Lance's gaze tracked the movement. His throat worked, and his own lips parted.

Gwin leaned into him. He held onto her, not turning away from her advance. But he did turn his head.

"We can't," he said. "Not here."

"There's no one around." She wanted to curse

the words the moment they left her lips. "That's not what I meant. I'm not ashamed of you, of what we have. As soon as we get home, I'm shouting it from the turrets."

In the darkening night, Lance's expression was clear. He gazed down at her with a soft expression that brimmed with love. His sigh was filled with appreciation.

"That's not what I meant." Lance swooped a strand of hair from the bridge of her nose and tucked it behind her ear. "We're out in the middle of nowhere. We're practically sitting ducks."

She relaxed, pressing her chest into his, wrapping her arms around his neck. "It could be worse."

The sound of the beating hearts grew louder. Instead of thumping, it sounded more like clicking and clacking. Like horses in a trot.

"You had to say *it could be worse*," Lance groaned. "Has Loren taught you nothing about horror movie clichés?"

The sound of hooves touched her ears. She looked over her shoulder to see two old horses. As their heads bobbed up and down, she caught sight of an elderly couple coming into view under the rising moonlight.

Lance remained vigilant, even though it was

clear there was no threat from the elderly duo. Gwin kept her promise to stay out of trouble and stayed within the cone of his protection. Really, she had no complaint of her current location.

"Having a little trouble there?" the elderly man called out in English with a thick, French accent.

He dismounted from the cart, coming around to hand down his companion. A cloud of silver-white hair floated from the cart to the ground. A matronly smile lit the night when the old woman lifted her head. She wrapped her hand around the arm of the old man, who Gwin had to assume was her husband.

The chivalrous gesture loosened Lance's stance. Gwin's own knight relaxed as the couple came near.

"This truck is older than me," said the man with a laugh. He was in blue overalls. He pulled his farmer's cap over his bald head.

"I've checked the oil and starter," said Lance

The farmer left the hood and walked to the driver's side. He looked in the window. "Did you check the gas? You're on E."

Lance scrubbed his hand over his face.

The man clapped him on his back. "There's a fuel station in town about five miles from here. But they're closed for the night. And I'm afraid there are no hotels or inns in the village."

"Why don't you come home with us? You can get cleaned up," said the woman. "We have a spare room. You can grab a bite and some rest."

"Do you have a phone?" asked Lance.

"Afraid not. But the service station does. You can make your call in the morning."

The farmer's wife took Gwin by the arm and led her to the cart. Her smile and earthy scent reminded Gwin of Igraine.

"Most young couples drive fancy cars through the countryside," said the older lady.

"We were visiting the Perceptory of Arville," said Gwin.

"The old knight? I knew him when I was a girl. My aunt fancied him. She kept a tender for him all these years."

"Is she still with us?"

The farmer's wife nodded. "She lives in the city. She'll celebrate her ninety-fifth birthday this year. She's just as spry as a fifty-year-old. How long have you two been together?"

"Feels like a hundred years," said Gwin looking to Lance.

"Must be newlyweds."

"Not yet," said Gwin. "But we are taking our vows soon."

25

———

The door shut behind them with a quiet snick. Lance prepared for the oncoming battle but knew he was ill-equipped to handle the onslaught. There was no more defense he could mount against this adversary.

The door closing sounded like a cell door slamming him into a confined place. He stared at the four-post apparatus inside the room that would torture him all night. He shouldn't have trusted that nice couple. They were making him face his deepest fear; being alone in a bedroom with Gwin.

No man could stand this test of chastity. Perhaps he could've withstood the test two days ago before Gwin had openly displayed her love for him and her intention to part ways with her husband.

Lance could have her. *One day* he could have her. But not *tonight.* Tonight she was still bound by the vows of her marriage.

He'd gone so far as to lust after another man's wife for decades. He'd broken his boundaries of embracing her, kissing her. But the bed is where he drew the line.

Despite what he'd said earlier, Lance still held those vows as a sacrament, a holy order that he would not break.

The floor would be just fine for him tonight. He deserved its hard planks. The problem was, he suspected Gwin held a different view of her vows, a view that would have them sharing the solitary, full mattress.

The elderly couple had assumed they were married. Gwin encouraged the notion all during the drive to their quaint cottage. As well as through the homemade dinner that was served.

Now Gwin sat at a vanity washing herself with water from a bowl. Sounds of water sluicing made him seek her. He watched her fingers as she squeezed the cloth. Water trickled over her hands, hands he'd felt the healing touch of for a century and the caress of for just a day. Lance had had wine at dinner, but he was thirsty again.

Gwin put the rag to her neck. She closed her eyes in relief as water lapped at the skin there. When she opened them, her gaze landed on him.

She didn't need words. He heard the plea in her command clearly. The traitor that he was, he left his post and went to her.

Lance took the rag from her hands and began to wash her. He moved the hair from her neck. He wiped away the dust of the road. He cooled the sun's warmth from her forehead. He wiped the smudges from the church fire from beneath her eyes. She'd healed him for decades, but now she was in his care.

He would not fail her. He would not take advantage of the situation, or her virtue like her husband had done their entire lives together.

"I've never been touched," she said.

"You've always been so busy caring for others."

"No. I've never been touched by my husband."

Lance's fingers stilled. Water dripped to the floor. Droplets splashed like waves crashing onto a pier.

"I've been living a lie. Merlin and I never consummated our marriage. He couldn't perform on the wedding night."

Lance had just managed to resurface after that tidal wave of information. Now the air left the room.

The world spun at this next admission. Gwin; a virgin?

"He didn't keep his vow?"

Gwin shook her head. Lance eyed her reflection in the mirror, but he needed to see the truth in her eyes. He dropped the wet rag with a plop to the floor. Taking her shoulders, he turned her to him.

"I've been holding onto a lie," she said. "There's nothing keeping us apart, no reason I can't be yours. I've never belonged to anyone else. I never wanted to. I've always been yours."

Lance's knees buckled. He rested his head on her shoulder as though he were the blade blessing her into sainthood.

"I don't want to live a lie anymore." She met his gaze. "I want to give myself to you. I want to give my vow to you. I've waited for decades. The world could end tonight. I won't wait any longer."

She tugged at the bottom of his shirt. It gave easily from his waistband. His mind was so befuddled that he was a puppet to her string pulling.

She tugged upward, and he lifted his arms. She struggled to get the shirt over his head. He ducked to give her access. She placed her hands on his chest. His heart beat double time for her.

Gwin was unclaimed. Words were one manner

of promise, but it was nothing without deeds. Gwin was unbound. Gwin could be his. Gwin could be his now, tonight.

He watched in a daze as she lifted the blouse from her head. Lance stared openly, unashamedly at two perfect globes. Her nipples strained the fabric of her bra eager for his touch.

Her hands moved to her jeans, twisting the fabric until the button gave. The cloth, which had hugged her every curve all day long, slipped off her body like a sigh, landing on the floor in a heap. There was nothing between them but her lace panties that matched her bra.

Gwin reached for the button of Lance's trousers. Her fingers uncertain but still bold as they coiled into the fabric to free him.

"Stop," said Lance.

The hazy cloud of uncertainty in her blue gaze darkened. "Please don't tell me you're impotent too?"

Lance choked on his response. "No, it's not that."

She snatched her hand away. "It's me, isn't it? There's something wrong with me?"

Lance could've kicked himself. She'd been denied the pleasure of touch for a century because of one inept man. Now, he was the one cocking everything up. "Gwin, you're perfect."

"Then why? You've been with others. I heard ladies talking."

"They lied," he said. "I've never touched them. I've never touched anyone."

Her brow drew with confusion. He couldn't blame her. It was a big admission. Something he'd never told anyone, especially not his brothers at arms.

"I was young when I came to Camelot. I'd seen the effects that sex without marriage could have on a woman and child. I knew I never wanted to bring that shame on anyone. And then I saw you. I never wanted to marry anyone but you."

"So ... you never ...?"

"I'm untouched, like you. I've never wanted anyone but you."

She flew into his arms. Her mouth assaulted his in a kiss that marked him, body and soul. Lance pressed her to him, arching her spine back to press her chest into his. He tilted her head back so that he could press his suit.

They drank from each other. Her soft moans a perfect harmony to his deep groans. Their hands moved up and down the other's body, playing each other like practiced instruments. It was a song they'd been humming for years. And now, finally, they'd get to sing it out loud.

He wasn't sure how they found themselves on the bed. It was inevitable. He'd known it the moment the door clicked behind them that this was where the night would end, with her in his arms. But it wasn't enough.

With great effort, Lance unraveled Gwin's arms from his neck and her legs from his torso. Despite her very vocal protests, he rose from her. Undoing the belt from his pants, he let the garment fall to the floor. The belt he kept a hold of.

Gwin's eyes widened as he rejoined her on the bed. Her gaze was trained on the belt and not on his erect flesh.

"Give me your hand," he said.

She did as she was told. Lance clasped her right hand with his left hand. Then he wove the belt around their wrists. It wasn't a cord or a ribbon, but it would do the trick.

"Repeat after me," he instructed. "*Lord, keep us to remember when we first met and the strong love that grew between us.*"

Lance began the words of the Scottish wedding prayer. Gwin faithfully repeated each of his words without missing a beat.

"To work that love into practical things so that nothing can divide us."

Lance bound the belt beneath their hands as Gwin repeated his words.

"We ask for words both kind and loving and hearts always ready to ask forgiveness as well as to forgive."

With the last loop of the belt, he fastened the buckle over the bracelet he'd given her earlier. It was a tight clench. He knew that neither of them would ever want to escape.

"Dear Lord, we put our marriage into your hands."

Gwin repeated the last of his words, tears brimming in her eyes.

"Now you're mine," he said, his voice just barely above that of a possessive animal marking his territory.

The few scraps of material that barred her from him were gone in an instant. And then she was bare. He'd ached for decades to know what was beneath her layers of fabric, dreamed of it in the dead of the night. Now he knew.

She was perfection. Her breasts rose to meet him. The hollow of her belly begged for kisses. The thatch of hair between her legs glistened, ready for him after all these years.

Lance was eager to get inside. But he knew he

had to take his time with her. Hell, he had to take his time with himself. This was a moment he never thought would come, and now that it was here he didn't want to embarrass himself.

But Gwin would have nothing for a slow seduction. She arched into him, rubbed him in all the right places, and then angled her hips until they found their union.

He couldn't deny either of them. He slipped inside with a welcomed ease. They held like that for long moments until they both caught their breath.

Lance looked down at Gwin. Like every moment of their lives, words were not necessary. It was crystal clear what she meant to him, and he to her. But Gwin decided she needed to speak her truth in this moment.

A possessive smile stretched across her face as she said, "And now *you* are mine."

26

Waking up was the last thing Gwin wanted to do. Her body felt languid and heavy from pleasure. She and Lancelot had made love all night long and into the morning.

Their first time, they'd both been in a hurry and things had escalated quickly. After that first time, they came together again. The second time was slow. They both spent time exploring the other, kissing every patch of skin, tasting every crevice.

Lance had spent an ample amount of time on both of her breasts. Gwin had squirmed and undulated until her body shook with a release. Then he'd entered her, pumping deep and long until she'd found another release alongside him.

They'd rested for a few hours, wrapped inside

each other's embrace. Then they'd join together again, seeking not only another release but the familiarity of each other that they'd been denied for so long.

This was the life she'd always wanted. The life she hadn't dared to dream could be hers. Lance had given her his vow, fastening their hands together, entering her body, and binding them for an eternity.

With that thought, she realized waking up to this new day, the first day of her new life, was an occasion for celebration. When she opened her eyes the sun's rays didn't greet her. Instead, fire did. Fiery, red hair and blue eyes so clear they rivaled the sky.

Lance's entire face was so bright as he looked down at her. His brows were tall peaks that sang her praises. His lips stretched wide, ready to take hers or whisper more vows. But he said nothing.

Like always they didn't need words between them. The truth of his love was clear. The heat of his desire was evident.

His hand idly caressed the flesh at her hips. Her fingers rested on his chest, playing in the fine hairs there. Those hairs weren't red upon closer examination. The hair on his chest was golden.

"One of us should say something," she whispered into the silence.

"You just did. What would you like me to say?"

"Tell me you love me."

"You know that. You've always known that."

"I've only heard you say it once," she said. "And you were cross with me at the time."

Lance slid his large palm down her back until it rested at her sacrum. He pulled her close until there was no breadth between their bodies. Gwin felt the strength of his erection, the heat of his body, the beat of his heart.

"I love you. I was born for the sole purpose of loving you."

She felt like she was going to burst. There was so much happiness inside of her. She wrapped her arms around his neck and tugged him down. But he leaned back.

"We have to get up, my love," said Lance. "We have to save the world."

"Can't it wait another hour?"

"You wanted to be a hero," he said pulling away from her. "This is a part of the job description."

Gwin watched him as he left the bed. She would've blushed to see a naked man that wasn't Merlin only a day ago. So much had changed in a day and a night.

She'd nearly died more than once.

She'd become a hero.

She'd lost her virginity.

And finally, she had the man of her dreams in her arms.

If the world did end today, she'd die a happy woman.

She immediately retracted that thought. If the world ended today, she would go kicking and screaming. One night was not enough.

Gwin left the bed. She washed Lance's body with the cold water from last night. With the cloth heated from his warmth, he washed her skin. They helped each other dress between kisses. Then they entwined their hands and left the room.

After a hearty breakfast, which the old couple insisted on, they drove them into the town square in their carriage. Lance went to get the gas, using cash from the couple which he insisted he'd pay back, while Gwin went inside to use the phone. The first ring barely finished before Morgan came on the line.

"Tell me you did the deed," said her sister.

Gwin expected her cheeks to flame, but they didn't. For years, decades, she'd listen as married women and widows talked in code about their amorous activities. Gwin had always remained silent and demure, politely declining to talk about her bedsport. Never letting on that there were no games being played in her bedroom.

Now, Gwin let out a very long, very deep, very telling sigh.

"That good?" Morgan squealed. "Go, sis!"

Gwin eyed Lance out the window of the storefront. She watched him move now realizing the power of that body. "Nope. Better."

"I'm so proud of you. I've gotta text Loren."

"Morgan, no."

"She's going to find out."

Now the dread spread through Gwin. She'd talked a good game about shouting from the rooftops about her relationship with Lance. But she knew that he still wanted discretion when it came to their newfound affair. "Are people talking? Do they suspect?"

Morgan snorted. "You, Miss Virtuous, and Lance, the Pinnacle of Chivalry? No. No one's said a word. And that's really sad. The only one that's even asked about you was the old ball and chain."

"How is he?" Gwin asked about her soon to be ex-husband.

"Dying," was Morgan's curt reply. "There's nothing anyone can do to save him. He's going to die whether you're here to tend to him or not. It's what he deserves."

"I know." She did know, and for the first time, she didn't feel the weight of responsibility on her shoulders. Instead, she looked again at Lance and his shoulders that she'd found comfort in, support in, love in.

Gwin had never had any of that with Merlin. She gave and he took. All their lives, Lance had given to her any piece of himself that he could pass along, and she'd done the same to him. Now, they would hold firm to each other out in the open.

"Take your time in Paris," said Morgan. "Everything's under control here. Go see the sights."

"We're not in Paris. We're just outside Arville. We went to the Perceptory there. We found Jacques de Molay's journals, the last Grand Master of the Original Order of the Templar Knights. Morgan, the curse, it's real."

"The stone curse?"

Gwin nodded, though she knew her sister couldn't see the gesture. "I cast it."

"You did?" Morgan's voice raised an octave like it did when she got excited about a new scientific find. "How? Tell me."

"Morgan, what this means is there are potentially hundreds of Templars frozen in stone."

"Do you know where?"

"They could be anywhere? Likely in Paris where they were imprisoned. We're headed back there now, back to Notre Dame."

"I'll tell Arthur. We'll meet you there."

"What do you think Arthur will do when we find them? Do we free hundreds of our enemies? Or do we leave them encased in stone?"

"I don't know?" said Morgan.

Neither did Gwin. What she'd read of de Molay's journals led her to believe that he was not corrupted by the crown and church. Maybe many of his followers were. There was the caveat that only one born with magic and in possession of the same metal that all swords of Camelot were wrought from. So, maybe they were all on their side.

Then again, her own magical husband had betrayed them all. They really had no way of knowing. She supposed they'd cross that bridge once they found them. Hopefully, they'd find those men before Malegant did.

27

The smell of gas fumes was in the air. No wonder with the five-gallon container in the bed of the truck. Lance wasn't taking any chances anymore.

The drive to Paris would take three hours. Shorter if he kept the pedal to the metal. But his foot kept easing off the gas as he relaxed into the comfortable silence with Gwin.

They'd never needed words. Now they didn't need glances, just this nearness. Their fingers entwined until he needed to maneuver the wheel with two hands. On the winding roads, she'd rest her hand on his knee until they reconnected.

His mind should've been on the mission at hand,

but it was squarely focused on his future with the woman beside him. His woman, his wife.

They'd exchanged vows and sealed the contract with deeds, again, and again, and then again. There would be no contesting this union.

"What wing will we take?" he asked. "The Galahad wing or the Lancelot one?"

Lance's hand covered Gwin's. As his fingers slid between the webbing of her pinkie and ring finger, his palm met with cold metal. They both stiffened as he grazed her wedding band.

Gwin unraveled her fingers from his. She rolled the car window down. Slipping the wedding ring off her finger, she tossed it out of the window.

With her bare fingers, she relinked their fingers and leaned into him. Her sigh of contentment rushed into his skin and settled into his heart. That was that.

"I don't care," she said scooting even closer to him. "I'll move into the stables if that's where you are."

"I'd be outnumbered in the Galahad wing."

Though Morgan spent her nights in Arthur's bed, there was still Loren. Lance had no desire to be awakened each morning to the discordant, electric tones of 80s music. Or worse, 90s music. Or even worse, John Hughes films on repeat. Dame Galahad was a pop cultist.

"I'm sure I'm the only lady in history to go from the Galahad wing to the Pendragon wing, only to go back to the Galahad wing and now I'll be in the Lancelot wing. I've striven to be a proper lady all of my life, a paragon of virtue. But I've turned out, by most standards, to be a whore."

Gwin's shoulders shook with laughter. The sounds of her giggles went over Lance's head. He'd been smacked hard in the face by her use of that harsh, improper word.

"That's not funny." Lance's tone was entirely devoid of humor. "I gave you my vow. I sealed it. This is not adultery."

"I know," Gwin soothed, her face turning sober and contrite.

"I don't want you tainted by my beginning."

"There is no taint on you. We've both spent our entire lives in pursuit of high ideals. We've sacrificed so much. I dare anyone to say a single negative word against us. In fact, Morgan told me not a single bit of gossip has been uttered about us being away together."

The mere thought of gossip about Gwin made Lance's insides quiver. He could handle the whispers about himself. His blood boiled to think they could be about her.

"Maybe we should wait until you are a widow," he said.

"I can't be a widow to a man who was never truly my husband. Besides," she took a deep breath and let it out on a shudder that lowered her voice to a whisper, "Even now, I might be pregnant with your child."

Lance's foot stomped down on the brake. They both jolted forward into the dashboard. "Oh, God. Are you okay?"

"Sure." Gwin rubbed at her chest. "Just your everyday bit of whiplash from my lover finding out he might be a dad."

Lance managed to steer them over to the side of the road. Once in park, he couldn't catch his breath. A child. There could be a child.

He looked up to see that they'd stopped beside a graveyard. All life beneath those stones was still. But there might be a new life growing inside of the woman he loved. If not now, then soon.

"Do you want a child?" she asked. Her voice was quiet. A little tremor quivered her lower lip. She bit at the trembling flesh with her tooth.

Lance lifted his hand to her face. He cupped her

chin and thumbed away the uncertainty from her lip. "I want everything with you. I want a grand wedding. I want a celebration that lasts for days. I want enough children to start an army."

Gwin smiled so wide and bright it caused another tremble. She overstretched her lips into a brilliant light of happiness. "Me too."

"But I want all of our children to be recognized by everyone. I want us to be legally married first."

Her overlarge smile snapped into a frown. Not one of disappointment. It was resignation. "Fine. All right."

Lance leaned forward to capture her lips. She tasted of happiness and hope. Before he could delve further into her, the prepaid phone he'd picked up at the town's gas station rang. He'd texted Arthur the number before getting on the road.

"We're in Paris," Arthur said through the speakerphone. "We just left the cathedral. What exactly are we looking for? Stone men?"

"There are a lot of statues all over this city," came Tristan's voice. "Mostly in graveyards."

"No, not statues," said Gwin. "When Lance and Sir Darvill were petrified, the stone formed around them."

"She's right," said Lance, remembering the stone

cold closing around him. "The markers will be tall, like a boulder with no form."

"Boulders?" Percy's gruff voice came through the line. "Like a stone circle?"

"There are no stone circles in Paris," said Arthur. "Only graves and gargoyles."

"Could it be a formation, like Stonehenge?" asked Percy.

"That wouldn't make sense," said Gwin. "Perhaps they're in England. There was something in de Molay's journal. About a parlay between the Templars and King Edward of England."

"That's not likely," said Arthur. "Edward seized much of the Templars wealth after the massacre. My grandfather and father spent many years getting magical artifacts back from both the British and French royalty."

"But de Molay mentioned the King in his journals," said Gwin. "He wrote that he'd sent an envoy to Carnac."

"Did he specifically mention the name of the king?" asked Arthur.

Lance watched Gwin's eyes fog over, going into her memory.

"No," she said.

"Do you think he was referencing your grandfather, Arthur the first?" asked Lance.

"It's possible," said Arthur. "Camelot and the original Templars were still in contact before the massacre. Though rifts had already been formed. There were still a few trusted Templars."

"You said Carnac," said Tristan. "There are thousands of stones there, some dating back to 3300 BCE. I remember reading tales of Pope Cornelius turning pagan soldiers into stone in the first century. Even some tales of Merlin turning people to stone."

"I've been to Carnac," said Percy. "I've seen those stones. They're not Sarsen. They're tall. Some are in straight, even lines. Like soldiers lining up."

There was a long pause of silence on both ends of the phone. Then everyone spoke at once.

"We need to get to Carnac."

28

———

Gwin's fingers dug into Lance's thigh. It wasn't a ploy at seduction, unfortunately. It was to hold on as he took one after another hairpin turn on the roads to Carnac.

Once again, they found themselves watching the sun tuck its rays beneath the horizon. They'd had to reroute their journey from Paris to Carnac, which was at the edge of Brittany just before the land fell into the sea.

There was no ley line access to the area that they knew of. Arthur and the others were making the same trek via vehicle across France. Since Lance and Gwin had to detour, the others would most certainly arrive first.

"When we get there," said Lance, "I need you to stay back."

They were within the city limits. The last few rays of the sun painted the horizon a shade between orange and red. To Gwin, it looked bruised and battered, but still a lovely sight.

"I understand," said Gwin. "But don't worry. If Malegant is there, he can't break the curse."

"No, he'd need a witch." Lance looked at her pointedly. "Which is why I need you to stay back. I'd rather put you up in a hotel. Or better yet, find a church on a ley line and send you home."

Gwin did not like that idea. "I'm not leaving you."

Lance opened his mouth to protest but she cut him off.

"Believe me, I've had enough adventure for a long while. I'll stay out of the way. I'll stay safe, I promise. But Lance, you realize nothing in our lives has worked out the way we've planned. I've spent too many days away from you. This won't be one of those days."

His jaw clenched. The muscle in his thigh tensed. But he didn't argue.

"Besides, Arthur, Percy, and Tristan will be there ahead of us. Four knights against whatever is left of Malegant's army is nothing."

Though when they pulled up, Arthur and the others weren't there. But there were hundreds of stones. It looked to Gwin like a sea of them, rising and sinking down on its own horizon.

Lance parked in the quiet village. Part of the town was a family seaside resort. It was after dark. So, most visitors and residents alike were inside for the night.

"There's magic here," said Gwin. "I can feel the energy."

Lance's hand tensed around hers. "At some point, the Templars turned on Camelot. What if these are the turncoats? What if they were mounting an offense against Camelot? It's just a boat ride across the Celtic Sea to Cardiff."

"We can't leave human beings trapped in stone for all time. They should at least be set free to meet their God-given end."

"More wounded souls for you to tend to in the infirmary?" There was an air of annoyance in his voice.

"Men aren't born bad. It's a decision they make and keep making every day until they change their minds."

Lance and Gwin were at the edge of the field where the town turned to what was effectively large gravestones if there were beings encased in the stones. Who knew if the men were even alive after hundreds of years? Just as Percy had said, the stones were lined up like soldiers, giants in neat formations.

Gwin put her hand to a tall boulder. It was faint, but she felt the pulse of magic within. Lance pulled her hand away. When he did, the jagged rock took a piece of his flesh leaving behind drops of blood on the rough surface.

"Let me see that." Gwin reached for Lance's wound.

Lance gave her his hand. She pushed her healing magic into him. It was a familiar gesture, but now she couldn't tell her energy from his. It was as though they were one.

Which was why she felt his apprehension before she heard the shuffle. Lance pulled her behind the boulders. Shadows moved in the dark. Voices carried.

Gwin was not surprised to find that she recognized them. They were the same two Templars from the Perceptory. And they still weren't happy with their new weekend job.

"This is utter bull shit," said the Doubter. "I'm done with traipsing around old homes and graves for this wanker. Stay if you want, but I'm out of here."

The two rounded the stones. There wasn't enough room to hide both her body and Lance's. The Templars looked from Lance to Gwin and back again. Then they looked at each other and grinned.

"Finally," said the doubting defector, drawing his sword. "Some action."

Lance reached for his brooch and released his sword. The men's confident smirks fell a bit. Lance didn't hesitate.

He lunged into the Doubter. The fight was over before it began as Lance disarmed the man who was apparently all talk and inept action. The Templar's sword went flying and landed at Gwin's feet.

Lance looked from the sword to Gwin, and back to the neutralized man. Lance's gaze blazed murder.

Before Lance raised his sword for the killing strike, the second Templar did the stupidest thing a man could do. He launched himself and his sword at Gwin.

Gwin ducked the man's advance. She bent down and grabbed the Doubter's discarded sword. She rose with the weapon in her firm grasp. With a parry and an overhaul strike, she had the second man disarmed and on his knees beside his partner.

"My grandfather was Sir Galahad," she said. "Do you really think he'd leave his daughters or granddaughters not knowing how to handle a sword?"

The men were mute. The Doubter openly wept. Gwin felt not an ounce of mercy.

"Where's Malegant?" said Lance.

Without hesitation or any semblance of loyalty, the two men pointed to the far side of the field.

"Please don't kill us," whimpered the Doubter. "We're not really on their side."

"You took the vows of the Templars?" Lance's blade was unwavering as it pointed at the man's heart.

"They were just words," whimpered the other man. "I'm just a banker. I wanted some excitement."

"I still live with my mum," said the other.

Lance didn't lower his sword. "Stand up."

The men sobbed and sniffled as they rose.

"Take off that tunic." Lance's growl was low and controlled. "You are a disgrace to the men who died protecting the true meaning of that cross."

The two men bared their chests. They handed over the white tunics. Lance made them turn the fabric inside out so that the red of the cross was muted.

"Now run into town and pray the authorities find you and not my brothers who are en route."

The two men took off running, tails between their legs.

Once the men were out of sight, Lance took hold of Gwin. He pulled her to him with one hand, loosening the sword from her grasp with the other. Gwin let him hold her, but she stood firm as she did so.

"Don't you dare send me away," she said. "Or leave me behind. Whatever happens to you, it happens to me too."

He didn't argue. He took her hand firmly in his own. They made their way quietly across the expanse of stones.

The magic got stronger and stronger the closer they got to the water. But no one was in the direction the men had pointed to. Had they been duped? Gwin was about to ask when a ringtone sang into the night. There was only one person that had the number.

Lance pulled the phone out of his pocket. He clicked the phone open. But then they heard another click.

Gwin knew that sound from being around a weapons room all of her life. It was the sound of a crossbow being loaded. The sound repeated through the air, at least half a dozen crossbows were loaded.

Lance put the phone to his ear. "I hope you're nearby."

"We got turned around," Arthur's voice was clear in the silent night. "We're in a bit of traffic. You guys there?"

"Yup. We're here. And we're not alone."

29

In the moon's light, Lance caught the glint of six sharp points aimed directly at his chest. The only reason he didn't fly into a blind fury was because all the arrows were aimed at him and not Gwin. Though all of the arrows held steady in their quivers, it didn't detract from the sharp pain in his heart.

These men were mostly novices. They were close range and would certainly hit their target if they loosed those arrows. Any of those arrows could quiver, miss their intended target, and hit Gwin. The thought caused his heart to beat so violently blood pushed at his veins to let loose its rage.

He needed to get her to safety. He needed to find a distraction that would allow her to take cover. Even as he thought it, he knew she would never leave his side.

They'd spent so much of their lives together apart. If this was going to be his last, she was coming with him. That was the depth of her loyalty to him. In the face of this danger, he wanted to turn to her and pull her into an embrace.

But he couldn't. Not because of the danger surrounding them. Because of her.

Gwin's hands were lit with witch fire. An angry, red fire that was not meant for healing. No, this fire would tear asunder any flesh that came near it.

God, he loved that woman.

Malegant tsked. "I'd put that out if I were you, my lady. Make it too hot and fingers get slippery."

The villain stalked forward between the large brawler of a man Lance had tussled with back in Champagne. Instead of a weapon, Malegant held an ancient tomb in his hands. It looked like a copy of the journal Gwin had found back in Paris. They must've left it out in the Arville Perceptory.

Did Malegant already have the words of the curse? He wouldn't be able to break it on his own. He'd need someone with magic to do it for him.

"Let her go," said Lance.

"You know I'm not going to do that. I need her

to free my brothers." Malegant raised his hands in the moonlight, lifting them up and indicating the stones surrounding them. "This army of hundreds of devout Templars came to the coast ready to cross and take on Camelot. Tonight, they'll be freed and that mission that began hundreds of years ago will finally see the light of completion."

The raging blood coursing through Lance's veins rushed to a stop. What if they'd gotten it wrong? What if these Templars hadn't been fleeing for help? What if they'd been mounting an attack?

Lance did the one thing he was taught to never do. He turned his back on his enemy and looked down into the face of his love. Gwin's determined chin was raised. She didn't believe Malegant's view.

Could Lance chance it? Better the devil he already knew? Or the one who may or may not be on his side?

"I'm not going to shoot the witch because I need her," said Malegant. "But I will have them shoot you if she doesn't do what I ask."

That was all it took. Gwin clenched her fists. The fire died out, but the red heat remained. She plastered on that fake smile he hated so much; the Hostess Smile, Morgan called it. It was the look she gave when she subjugated her happiness and comfort for others.

She was going to do it. She was going to break the curse and free the Templars. Lance reached for Gwin as she took a step.

The glint of arrows nearly blinded him as they raised up and at him. The desire to pull her close into his protection warred with the need to shove her out of danger.

Gwin reached over and unfurled his fingers from her forearm. She smiled up at him. So much was communicated in that one glance.

I love you.

Don't worry about me.

I really wish I could kiss you right now.

I've got this.

He wasn't so sure if she did have this. He didn't have any of it under control. Once those Stone Templars were free, there was no guarantee whose side they'd be on. They'd have hundreds of confused warriors coming out of stone, with swords in hand. It would be chaos.

Speaking of swords, Lance unfastened his brooch and dropped it to the ground at his feet. Whether she was able to break the curse or not, he was not about to be turned to stone and leave her completely unprotected.

Gwin took a deep breath. Lance felt her inhalation all the way down into the pit of his stomach. They exhaled together. His breath was anxiety-ridden. Hers was confident. She had every belief this would work out for them. He hoped she was right.

She spoke the words. And ... nothing.

The wind whistled, rustling a few blades of grass and turning over a pebble or two. The heavy breathing of a few of the untried Templars could be heard over the strain of holding a taut bow for so long. That left Lance less fearful of what would come out of the stones and more cautious of the weary arms all around them.

Gwin took another breath and said the words again. Night creatures raised their voices to hers in chorus. But no stone turned.

Did the curse have a time limit? Was it now irreversible? Or had there never been any men encased within those stones to begin with?

Out of the corner of his eye, Lance saw a few bows lower. The part-time Templars were a bit away from him, but he felt the same doubt from a few of them that had been seething in the two defectors who'd run off into the town. The rest of these men were losing faith in their leader.

One glance at Malegant told Lance the man wasn't the least concerned about his life. Malegant's mind was focused on the Stone Templars and their lack of arrival. But unlike Lance, Malegant's doubt was only momentary. He turned a cold gaze on Gwin.

"If the hag wants to play games, I'll play too," he snarled. "Shoot him."

Unfortunately, for Malegant just as his stone army was stiff, his living army was also not at the ready. Unlike Lance.

Lance shoved Gwin to the ground with one hand and grabbed his brooch with the other hand. A flick of his finger turned the piece of jewelry into a sword. A flick of his wrist sent that sword into the gut of the large brawler whom Lance assumed was the best shot and the most alert.

The brawler hadn't yet hit the ground by the time Lance was up and gunning for two more Templars. Behind him, Lance felt the heat of witch fire at his back. He didn't need to turn to know that Gwin was putting a blaze to the Templars on the other side of them.

Lance went for the shins of one Templar,

knocking him down with one blow. Then he lifted the man's sword as he came to stand, slicing upward and relieving the guts of the man who'd stood at his right. Three men down. Just three to go, depending on how Gwin had done with her adversaries.

When Lance came to standing, pride filled his heart to see the other two Templars had been blasted back a dozen feet with witch fire. They were either unconscious or no longer with the living. He didn't care which. He only cared that Gwin was whole.

That left only one Templar. Malegant. As if he heard his name being whispered, the man reappeared.

There was no one left to fight his battles. All of his toy soldiers were fallen. And the stone ones he was relying on were either forever encased in stone or had never been there to begin with. He was done.

Only he wasn't.

Lance cursed himself for not seeing it coming. Malegant's son, Accolon, had pulled the same trick with Morgan. From a charm around his neck, Malegant produced a locket. Before the villain opened it, Lance knew what was inside that locket.

The fire died out of Gwin's hands, and she fell to her knees.

Lance tried to run to her, but moving against a Sarsen stone was like moving through quicksand. A blade glinted beside the stone. Malegant produced a dagger and held it at Gwin's neck.

Gwin turned her gaze to Lance. There was no fear. Neither was there resignation. Gwin's eyes shone with a love so pure, so sure, so bright that it blinded Lance. He sank to his knees, partly out of weakness. Mostly out of devotion to this woman.

"I love you," said Gwin.

Lance opened his mouth to say the same, but the sound of a blade cutting into flesh tore through the air. The sickening sound was followed by a scream. The scream was a masculine one, not a feminine one.

Lance shifted his gaze from Gwin's face to the blade that had been at her neck. It was no longer there. Neither was the hand that had held it. Nor the arm that belonged to the villain. Malegant's arm was on the ground. Blood dripping from his shoulder.

A Templar soldier lifted his sword and placed it to Malegant's neck. "You dare threaten a lady."

It wasn't a question. It was a sentence. The chivalric code held that no knight ever raised his hand or his blade to a lady, even if she were a foe. The penalty was death.

"No," Malegant whimpered. "She's a witch."

"You would dare harm a sacred child of God?" said the man. No, not man. He was a Templar. But not one of the toy soldiers from modern day. His clothing was that of the original Templars. The cross emblazoned on his chest was two unadorned lines. No hooks, triangles, or arrows of modern day. The red covering his chest was a true cross. "You are no man."

Malegant opened his mouth to protest, but the Templar's sword separated his head from the rest of his body.

Lance looked up to see other Templars coming out of their stones. But not all came out alive. Some keeled over and died on the spot right before their eyes. Lance couldn't come to their aide. Another sword was pointed at his throat.

eath. Death was all around Gwin. It clawed at her skin, threatening to pull her into its stone cold depths. The smell of it rose and fell inside her like the tide, sending her internal sense of balance off. The taste of it clutched at her throat, but she dared not swallow the lump that formed there.

When she'd broken free of one tendril of darkness, another would reach up and ensnare her. It would whisper that sleep would be easier than fighting. Just a moment's rest in the ice cold, crashing waves and the pain would stop.

She was tempted. She was so tempted to close her eyes to the dead bodies all around her. The dead bodies of Templars falling out of their stone prisons and into pain-filled deaths.

She was tempted to ignore their cries of pain. The agony of men who emerged from their rock graves with breath in their lungs but confusion in their heads. She couldn't heal them all. But she had to try. She was the only one who could, and she was failing them.

Gwin unfurled the cold dead fingers of the man at her feet. His fingers cracked as she loosed his hold. As death claimed the men, the Templars turned back to stone. Some of them crumbled into broken rock after their final transformation. Gwin got to her feet as another man cried out in pain.

"That's enough, Gwin. There's nothing more you can do."

Lance's warm arms came around her, stopping her advance. The moment they did, they breathed new life into her. She felt invigorated. She could do this with him by her side. She could save a few more.

"No," he said firmly. "They're gone. Those men weren't born with enough magic in their bloodline to keep them alive in the curse for this long. You won't give your life away again to heal someone who is already lost. I won't let you. I love you too much."

She knew he was right. There was nothing more she could do, save pour out her magical soul. Even then, many men would still die. Already dozens lay dead, their flesh hardening and crumbling to stone. While a few others gasped one last breath before their hearts hardened again. Permanently this time.

Less than two dozen made it out alive with beating hearts.

"We've been here for over seven hundred years?" said Sir Rex. He was the first knight to emerge, the one who'd saved Gwin's life from Malegant.

Rex, the Resilient, he'd called himself as he stared down at Lance and judged him from the end of his blade. Luckily, Rex had read Lance correctly and saw that the man was an honorable knight of Camelot.

Rex had lowered his sword and come to his knee. Not out of deference. But because he'd been weak. The other men followed soon, falling out of the stones and either dying or clinging to life.

"What's the last thing you remember?" asked Arthur.

Arthur, Percy, and Tristan had arrived in the midst of the coming out party. Arthur sat down beside Rex, offering the man a bottled water.

Rex stared at the plastic. He winced as he squeezed the bottled and it crackled. He took a swig and then a gulp.

Sir Rex looked to be around Author's age, early thirties by human standards. The rest of the survivors looked relatively younger.

They were mostly sitting amidst the rubble of rock, staring out or up. They were all shell-shocked from their long imprisonment. Many appeared afraid to move. Others kept moving and massaging their limbs as though that would stave off rigor mortis.

Gwin wanted to reach out to them. Instead, she did as she was told and stayed inside Lance's embrace.

"There was so much corruption within the Order in its final days," Rex said after he'd quenched his thirst. "We managed to evade King Phillip and Pope Clement's massacre only because we were in the East at the time on a mission. We went about finding the true believers for two years. It was hard to know who to trust when we returned. We attempted to rescue the Grand Master, but we failed. De Molay got word to us. He told us he had a way out and for us to head to Camelot to seek refuge. He pressed that we were to never let down our weapons. We were at Carnac waiting to cross when it happened."

"The curse?" said Arthur.

"One moment we were marching toward the waters, and the next ..." Sir Rex rubbed his arm. "Everything just stopped. I couldn't move. I could hear and see everything around me. After a while, the fight went out of me, and I just stood still. I didn't know such dark magic existed."

"He was trying to save you," said Gwin. "He was trying to keep you hidden. Something must have gone wrong."

"Yeah," said Arthur. "His execution."

"I still don't know how the Grand Master was able to curse us," said Sir Rex.

Gwin nearly said that de Molay had saved them, but she bit her tongue before the words could escape. As she did, she tasted blood and dust on her tongue. The blood was her own. The dust was that of the decrepit bodies of the fallen.

"Your swords," said Gwin. "They are all the same steel of the magical swords of Camelot."

Each man's blade glistened in the moonlight, vibrating with the same magic that ran in their bones.

"You are all descendants of witches and wizards," Gwin continued. "It's why you survived. Every living thing has a little magic in them. It's what we're all made of. But you all have more than most."

Rex's jaw went taut. His gaze hooded as though hiding something.

The man at Rex's right looked doubtful. Teodbald, the Blue, he'd called himself. "My mum is a farmer's wife. Was ..."

Teodbald looked back toward the town and its bright lights of electricity. He jerked as a plane flew overhead. Then made the sign of the cross over his chainmail.

"She plowed fields alongside my father her whole life," he said, after his silent prayer. "There was no magic in my home. You must be mistaken, my lady."

Gwin knew the man was wrong. It was faint, but she felt the magic in his blood. She felt the magic in all of the survivors' blood. They were all sons of Camelot. They just didn't know it.

"We've come for you now," said Arthur. "We'll take you home to Camelot to heal and figure out what to do next."

"What of the rest of the order?" said another Templar. "What became of them?"

"The Order is not what you remember," said Arthur. "The corruption spread. The original Knights Templar ranks were decimated. You are the last of your kind."

The silence was deafening. Even the stones underfoot were silent as the men realized their fate.

Figures moved in the distance towards them. The weary knights came up on shaky legs. A dozen swords drew to the ready.

"At ease, men." The Templars instantly responded to Arthur's commanding tone.

Percy and Tristan emerged from the darkness. They'd gone to charter a boat to cross the channel and had met with success. Even though it was late at night, money would rouse anyone from their bed, and the Knights of Camelot had plenty of funds. Gwin knew, she did the books.

After some cajoling, they piled the Templars into two trucks parked at the road and headed toward the water. Gwin sat in the front seat, sandwiched between Percy in the driver's seat and Lance at the passenger window.

"So ..." said Percy. "What's new?"

Gwin and Lance stared over at the knight.

She felt Lance's exhaustion alongside her own. Neither of them was in the mood for Percy's antics.

"I don't know..." Percy continued. "There's something different about you two? You look mature somehow. New haircut?"

They both decided to ignore the knight. Percy could be tactless. It was easier just to pretend they didn't hear him than to indulge him.

Percy snorted as if to tell them this was far from over.

They parked at the dock and unloaded. Percy and Tristan had chartered a ferry that could easily fit them all. They all climbed on board and Tristan, the son of a Norseman, took the boat's helm.

"Go below and get some rest," Arthur ordered the Templars.

Although Sir Rex was the clear leader of the men, the man had no qualms about listening to Arthur. As the leader of Camelot, Arthur outranked him. The Templars marched below as though they were headed off to battle. In a sense they were. It was a new world they'd face in the light of the new day.

Rex watched his men go below. Before he followed, he turned to Gwin. "Thank you, my lady. For finding us, releasing us, and for the gift of your healing power."

And with a bow, he left.

"Gwin," said Arthur, "Take the main cabin. You need the rest."

Like Rex, Gwin did not argue with her leader. She reached down and laced her fingers with Lance. She gave a tug but Lance didn't budge.

She looked up to find Arthur's brow raised at their connection. The leader of Camelot, Lance's best friend, the man who was both of their boss, their commander-in-chief whose respect they cared most about, tilted his head in what could only be read as disapproval at their union.

Gwin's heartbeat at the base of her throat. The thuds knocked her chin up in defiance. The pounding opened her throat to shout her love for Lance as loud as she could. But she went mute at the look on Lance's face.

She'd seen that look more times than she cared to count. It was the face she'd seen when his father had called him a bastard. It was the look she'd catch when the few unkind citizens of Camelot whispered as he walked by. Just as much as her heart beat loudly, she felt the tightening of Lance's chest in the face of this predicament.

She prepared herself to release her hold on him. She took a deep inhale, readying her chest to slink into itself when he let her go. Then she gave another tug, this time of her own hand and not his.

Lance jerked, as though being awakened from a nightmare. He glared down at their still entwined hands, as though looking for a foe. Seeing none, he glanced up at her, confusion on his brow.

"Did you think I would leave you?" His voice quaked with emotion.

Gwin relinked her fingers with his. She wrapped her free hand around his forearm. Though she felt the tremor in his hand, Lance's hold on her was absolute. When he spoke again his voice did not waver.

"Good night, Arthur. We'll see you in the morning."

And with that, Lance turned them both around. He walked on sea legs even though they were still docked. Once behind the closed door of the cabin, he slumped against the frame.

"You okay?" she asked.

He'd been looking down at the floor. Suddenly, blue eyes arrested her. Lance's gaze upon her made her pounding heart stop. There was something predatory about his stare. It was something primal.

"I would never abandon you," he said in a voice that wasn't his own. "I am not my father."

"I know," she tried to soothe.

"Even if I could not touch you, I would never leave your side. I gave you my vow."

"And I gave you mine. I'm yours."

"You're mine."

He took a step toward her. Something in his gaze made her gasp. Gwin's fight or flight responses told her to flee. She doused that instinct with witch fire. With her magical fire out, a more primal need took over.

Lance caught her lips with his. His kisses before had been gentle, careful. This kiss claimed her body and soul.

His hands were everywhere. On jean buttons, on shirt hems, on elastic bands of panties. In a blink, she was naked and beneath him. In a breath, he was sheathed inside of her. Then her entire world began to rock.

Gwin had no idea if it was the boat. She didn't care. She undulated beneath Lance, beside Lance, on top of Lance. He was no longer hiding, not from anything or anyone as he pressed his body into hers.

His cries of passion would easily be heard above deck. Gwin's moans of ecstasy would easily reach across the waves to be heard. When they both reached their climax, it would no doubt be clear to all on board—hell, all across France and England—what they were doing, what they had done, and what they meant to each other.

They were together. And now everyone knew it. Nothing could break them apart.

31

It wasn't quite dawn when wakefulness tugged at Lance's attention. He didn't open his eyes. He kept them closed as he waited for the weight of shame to hit his chest.

There would be no escaping it. Everyone on board would have heard what he and Gwin had gotten up to last night. Everyone would know about their affair.

Their adultery.

Lance didn't so much as hear the word as see it flash across his mind's eye. Only the light wasn't glaring. It was soft, more of a shadow than a light really. And it faded so quickly, he questioned if he'd actually seen it at all.

His chest felt light, free of any constrictions. His

heart beat a steady rhythm, no skipping about or accelerating. His mind was clear, alert.

Lance opened his eyes to a dark room, but he saw clearly. Blonde hair shimmered across his chest. One of Gwin's legs was thrown across his thighs.

Looking down, Lance saw the lush curve of her ass. His own hand rested at the fleshiest part of that curve. Like it was the most natural thing in the world.

Because it was the most natural thing in the world. Shame and guilt had no place in this bed. Adultery was an antonym to what lay between them.

For all intents and purposes, Gwin was his wife. He'd given his vow and staked his claim, as medieval as that sounded. But it was the way of things. And soon, right now, in fact, everyone would need to know that she was rightfully his.

Gwin shifted in his arms. Lance brought her closer to him, erasing the few millimeters of space that dared separate them. She didn't stir when he pressed a kiss into her hair. She didn't rouse as he extracted his body from hers. She didn't wake as he went through the task of dressing.

With the last button in its catch, Lance took another moment to smile down at Gwin. She clutched at the pillow he'd vacated. Her porcelain skin glimmered in the dark room. His eyes traveled up the pale pink of her toes, over her slim calves, lingered on the treasure that was her behind, before fighting hard to tear his gaze away from the pink nipple of her right breast.

If he wanted to, he could return to the bed and capture that breast. He could take her lips. He could undo his pants and sink back into the wonder of her.

But he didn't. Not now. There was no rush. He could be with her later, once they returned home safely and figured out how to explain their union to everyone.

First, he had to explain it to the most important person. Lance opened the door as quietly as possible and closed it with a snick. To his ears, that quiet snick sounded loud. His senses went on high alert. His senses told him that danger lurked around the corner.

Lance fingered the brooch pinned to his shirt. He knew with three other knights and a couple dozen Templars on board, that this was the second safest place in the world. The logic didn't assuage his anxiety. Something wasn't right.

Stepping up into the fresh air, he saw that the coast was in sight. However, the land seemed higher on the horizon than it should be. Water lapped against the side of the ship. Spray from a few of the waves splashed at his boots.

Before he could ponder it, something parted from the shadows. Lance reached for his sword but immediately stayed his hand.

"A word."

Lance sighed. He'd known this was coming last night when Arthur had raised his brow as Lance and Gwin walked off together. Originally, Lance had hoped The Talk would wait until they were back on dry land. Maybe even a few days after they were home.

But no. It would happen now.

Arthur and Lance walked a few steps away from the cabin. Arthur's footfalls were heavy, much like a church bell calling out the hour of doom. Up ahead, Lance spied Percy and Tristan trying and failing to look inconspicuous so that they might eavesdrop.

It was easy for many to believe that women was a gossipy lot, but they had nothing on the knights and squires of Camelot. Gathering, honing, and aiming the right bit of hearsay about another man could easily do more lasting damage than an injury from a blade.

Men didn't gossip for something so simple as power over each other. No, they slandered to embarrass, to annoy, and to humiliate in perpetuity. This set-down that Lance was about to receive would spread around the circle of the Round Table before they touched land.

"What were you thinking?" Arthur growled when they'd moved a sufficient distance from the cabin where Gwin still slept peacefully after a night of vigorous devil-may-care lovemaking.

"I was thinking that she is the love of my life," Lance offered. "That she is my life."

Arthur pushed his hands through his hair. Before he could get out any more admonishments, Lance continued.

"I have been nothing but honorable my entire life. I have stood by while the woman I love has been used by the entire town for her abilities. I have stewed in silence as she's been wrung dry by your brother."

"My brother; her husband. They took those vows and promised to stand by them."

Lance wanted to shout the truth; that those vows, that promise, had never been fulfilled. But it wasn't his truth to tell.

So, he'd let Arthur think the worst of him. He'd let everyone believe what they would. He no longer cared. The only person whose opinion he cared about was down the hall, and she knew the whole truth.

"I know how you feel about her," said Arthur. "Hell, everyone knows how the two of you feel. But she made a choice long ago, and she has to stand by that choice until death."

Lance grit his teeth. He'd said the same thing to Gwin only a day ago. That they could be together when Merlin died. But that leech was holding on to life with everything he could. At this rate, it would be another century before she was free.

"Look," said Arthur. "I'm Team Lance and Gwin. Or, Gwince? Or is it Lawin?"

The popular modern notion of merging two individuals' names together had to be Morgan's idea. She had deemed herself and Arthur Morghur. The name, fortunately, had not stuck. Lance doubted Gwince or Lawin would be very popular either.

"But you know how this looks," said Arthur. "After your father—"

"Lance is not his father." Gwin appeared at the side of the boat. Her hair was mussed, her clothing rumpled. The always poised Lady of the Castle looked as though she'd been tousled good. Lance couldn't hide the carnal smile of pride from his face.

"And I'm not married," she said as she marched up to Lance and Arthur.

She took Lance's arm and laced her fingers with his. Blue eyes shone up at him with a love so bright it nearly knocked Lance off the side of the boat. He felt the spray of the water tickle the backs of his shins.

"Not married?" Arthur frowned down at Gwin. "What are you talking about?"

Gwin took a deep breath, and then she spilled the awful truth. "My marriage with Merlin was never consummated. Your brother couldn't get it up."

"Ahh, Gwin!" Arthur groaned, closing his eyes and turning away from any knowledge of his brother's sex life.

In the distance, Percy and Tristan snickered. Even though Merlin wasn't a knight or a warrior in any sense, this was still good fodder for the game room.

"So, you see," Gwin continued, "Merlin never kept his vows. Not any of them."

Her chin had been high during the declaration. Now it dipped. Lance felt a shiver go through her body as she took a breath to begin her next confession.

"I've been living a lie. I've never truly been the Lady of the Castle. I don't deserve that title."

Arthur's face went through a number of emotions in a few seconds. From anger, to grossed-out, to surprised, and finally to compassion. "What are you talking about? You are the best thing that's ever happened to the castle. The entire town would fall apart without your leadership."

"But the covenant, the spell that binds my magic with the Pendragons and Tintagel, it never truly manifested because there was no true bond. Don't you see; I've kept the whole town in danger for a century by living this lie. We had the only ever breach last year because of me."

Now Lance went through a myriad of emotions. He never knew she felt this way, that she felt this level of responsibility.

"Gwin," Arthur took her hands in his, "we had a breach because Merlin betrayed us. He betrayed his wife, his family, and his entire people. That is not your fault. You are a treasure to us all. Your strength heals and soothes all who come in contact with you. Lance is right. If anything, it is all of us who have failed you. My family, in particular, put Merlin's health and wellbeing above your own. For that, I am ashamed."

"Well," she bit at her lower lip. "I'll forgive you if you'll forgive me."

Gwin stepped into Arthur's arms. He gave her a squeeze and a peck on the forehead. But she wasn't done.

"And Lance," she said. "You'll forgive Lance, too."

Arthur turned his glare back to Lance. "Lancelot still took advantage of an innocent."

"He didn't take advantage of me," said Gwin. "I've been trying to seduce him for days. And besides, we were both virgins until two nights ago."

"Ahh, Gwin!" Now it was Lance's turn to groan.

He closed his eyes and turned away from his leader and his brothers as his face turned redder than his hair. It didn't save him from the sounds of Lance and Percy guffawing with mirth. This bit of gossip was gold and would be aimed at him repeatedly for the next century.

Gwin threw up her hands. "Men."

The sun was rising higher on the horizon. A horizon that was a bit askew. Lance's entire world was off balance now with his heart so full of this woman. His feet were no longer firmly on the ground and he felt himself rocking in place with the pounding of his heart.

He'd been caught bedding the woman he loved,

the woman he would spend the rest of his life with. Lance pulled Gwin into his arms but frowned when he saw that he didn't have her full attention.

"Men," she repeated. "Where are the men? Where are the Templars?"

Lance looked down toward the passageway that would lead them below deck where the Templars had spent the night. His feet sloshed around in water that was at least an inch high and rising. He noted that the boat wasn't moving forward. It felt like they were sinking.

There should not be this much water on the floorboards. The others noted it too. Just as Lance and Gwin hadn't often needed words during their lives, Lance and his brothers-at-arms didn't need them during times of crisis.

They looked up at each other soundlessly. Without a word, they each drew their swords from their magical hiding places. As a unit, they all moved toward the entryway to the lower decks.

They went down below, but they didn't get beyond the door. Boulders blocked their way. Wrenching the door open, they saw that dozens of boulders blocked their way as water seeped out of the room.

32

Gwin stood on dry land, but she was soaked through. The last bit of warmth she'd had was about an hour ago when Lance had lifted her out of the dingy, wrapped her in a dry blanket, and sat her down on a private pier in the docks. The sun rose higher in the new day's sky as she watched the ferry filled with petrified men coming closer and closer.

Arthur was onboard the tugboat that pulled their boat from the water. Percy had returned with a crane to get the boulders out of the sinking ship. Tristan pulled up with a few of the town's witches. The women set about casting an illusion spell to keep the nosy humans away while Lance backed a semi-truck into the parking lot that they would use to load the Stone Templars onto and take them all to Camelot to determine what to do next.

Gwin took a moment to close her eyes. She was beyond exhausted. Not just a physical exhaustion. She was mentally and emotionally tired. Had it only been a full day since she'd been home?

Gwin had spent the last hour working her magic to keep the boat from sinking. She'd lifted tons of water, moving it up and over the side of the boat. But it was a losing battle with the weight of the Stone Templars in a vessel that wasn't built to carry their weight.

She'd changed tactics and focused her magic on the Templars. She could still feel the life of the men in the stones. But no matter how many times she said the words to break the curse, not a single stone cracked.

It was cruel. After a few hours of freedom, the men were all trapped again. Gwin felt the responsibility weigh on her shoulders like a dozen tons of stone. Though she was flesh and blood, her limbs were as heavy as rocks, her skin colder than stone, her heart a hollowed crag.

She closed her eyes, trying to breathe in the sun's warmth. Miraculously, warmth infused her. She opened her eyes to see Lance. She didn't see his face.

Just the side of his chin and his forearms holding her to him.

Gwin sighed into his touch as he lifted her. She turned her face into the space between the underside of his chin and the column of his neck as he carried her. He was sweat and salt and musk and the only place in the world she wanted to be.

She had no idea where he was taking her, and she didn't care. Not so long as they were together. If last night had taught her anything, then it was this; there was nothing and no one that would keep them apart from this day forward.

One hundred years had been too long to live a life as cold as stone. She would revel in his soft flesh for the rest of his days. He was the reason her heart beat, and she would no longer keep that pounding silent.

Lance sat her down on a soft cushion inside a cocoon of warmth. She opened her eyes to see that she was in the cab of the semi-truck with the heat and seat warmer on.

"Sleep."

He whispered the word like a spell. And it worked. She was out in a second. Her sleep was dreamless but fitful.

When she opened her eyes again, she felt as

though she'd slept for a weekend. She felt rejuvenated and ready to take on any challenge that came to them.

"There you are!"

And just like that, Gwin felt exhausted again. She was still cocooned inside the blanket wrapped around her. Still curled up in the heated passenger seat of the semi-truck.

But the scenery was different. Different but familiar. They were home, back in Camelot in the town square.

The driver's side of the truck was empty. The passenger door wrenched wide open, and Gwin stared down into the face of her mother. The displeased face of her mother.

Lance came up behind her mother. "I beg your pardon, my lady."

Gwynfhar glared at Lance. Once again, like he did last night under Arthur's glare, Lance hesitated. But only for the briefest of seconds.

He moved past her mother and reached out his hand to Gwin. Gwin allowed him to hand her out of the truck. Once she was on the ground, he didn't let go of her hand. He twined his fingers with hers. Gwin relaxed into his strong shoulder as she faced her mother.

The setting sun backlit her mother, casting severe shadows beneath Gwynfhar's narrowed gaze. Her mother's look was stormy. It should've cowed Gwin, but it didn't. Nothing could affect her now that she was living the life she wanted with the man she wanted.

"Your husband has taken a turn for the worse," said her mother.

Not even that. "There's nothing more I can do for him, Mother. I've given him more than enough of myself."

"You're his wife, the Lady of the Castle. You can go and be by his side. That is your duty."

"Actually it's not." Gwin gripped Lance's hand. Now was the time. The truth was coming out, starting with her mother. "Mother, you should know—"

"They're waking."

They all turned at the sound of Arthur's voice. He was at the back of the truck along with the other knights and the witches who'd come from the port. The doors of the truck were open and witch fire illuminated the inside where the setting sun didn't reach.

And there they were. The Stone Templars

gasped for breath. They reached free of their stone cages.

Gwin left the comfort of Lance's arms and her mother's glare to help the men. She went first to Sir Rex; he was bent over helping another of his men.

"I didn't sleep last night," he said. "None of us did. At the first ray of the sun, we began to turn. It took us over before we could call out for help."

"It's a heart spell," said Gwynfhar. She came up beside Rex, running her hand over the man's heart. "It's old magic. It's settled into their very being. The only thing that can break it permanently is another's heart."

"A blood sacrifice?" asked Gwin. The horror in her voice matched the dismay she saw in the eyes of the Templar soldiers.

"No, I mean a love spell," said her mother.

Gwin had never heard of such magic. The first thing a child learned as a young witch or wizard was that they couldn't compel someone to fall in love with them. They could get them to do what they wanted for some time. But love was its own magic.

"What do you mean a love spell, Mother?"

"They each need to find their true love," Gwynfhar said. "Only she will have the power to break the spell permanently."

The Templars had looked blanched as they'd come out of the stony cages. Now they all turned green at the mention of love and permanence.

"There may be a different way," said her mother. "It may not have to be true love. Chivalric love might do the trick. In their time, that was considered true love. It might work."

"So, if they all focused their love on one noble lady, the spell could be broken?" asked Arthur. "But what lady?"

Gwynfhar turned to her daughter. "Why, the noblest Lady of the Castle, of course."

33

It wasn't the pressing crowd of townsfolk trying to get a look at the Templars that had Lance short of breath. It wasn't the agony and confusion of the weary soldiers, gasping and crying out in pain as they came out of their stone captivity that caused his fingers to clench into impotent fists. It wasn't even the cold glare Lady Gwynfhar sent his way that caused the shiver to run down his spine as he retreated. It was the indecision on Gwin's brow that sent Lance into a back-walking retreat.

She was going to agree to her mother's plan. She had to agree. Otherwise, dozens of men would suffer every day when the sun came up.

There was no one else in the town who could do

it. Aside from Morgan, who'd just recently gotten her powers back, Gwin was the strongest witch in town. Only she had the magic in her veins to stave off the stone curse.

Gwin looked from the Templars to her mother, and then to the rising moon. She closed her eyes and retreated into herself. Lance felt the weight of the world that had just landed on her shoulders. He made a new vow. He would be there beside her to take on this added weight.

Once again, their love would have to wait. But it couldn't take as long this time. Maybe a decade at most to find all of the Templars their true loves so that their curses could be broken permanently.

Just ten years instead of a hundred. He could wait that long. He would wait forever for her.

But just as he turned to go, he saw Gwin back away from her mother. She was shaking her head in defiance of her mother's edict. She looked up, searching the crowd until she found and held his gaze.

"Gwin."

Her mother's voice was stern, but it didn't pull her attention away from Lance. Gwin's brows dipped down as they took Lance in. Lance heard Gwin's silent query clearly.

Did he truly think she'd choose someone, anyone, over him after everything they'd been through over the past couple of days, over the last century?

No. No, he didn't think she would choose. But he did believe that she would do her duty if called.

"Gwin," her mother tried again. "It is your duty."

"No," she said. "It's not."

Lance's hands were clenched into fists. His right fist rubbed over his heart. His spine was stiff in readiness. He took deep breaths as he waited for Gwin to say it, to reveal what they had always been to each other, what they were now.

"I'm not the Lady of the Castle," Gwin began.

As she prepared to throw off the cape of her century-old disguise, she kept her gaze locked onto his for strength. He saw that actually saying the words were proving harder than she anticipated.

Lance strode toward her. People instinctively parted out of his way, making a clear path so that he could get to her.

"Merlin and I never consummated our marriage. The vows never took hold."

There was a moment's silence as the people around her processed what she'd said. Then slowly, just as the water had crept onboard the ferry last night, the whispers started. Lance heard his name mixed with hers. The whispers buzzed around him like bees as he came closer and closer.

"There's someone else ..."

Lance caught sight of Lady Minerva who had propositioned him just days ago. The look on her face was one of *I told you so*. He heard the word *bastard, adultery, infidelity, affair*.

He was almost to Gwin, she was nearly in his grasp, but his feet stopped moving. His hands fell to his sides.

Lance lifted his gaze from hers. He looked around at the people he'd spent the last century protecting, risking his life for, whose approval he'd tried to win. With their gazes heavy upon him, he felt like a specimen under a microscope, a character under a spotlight. Worse of all, he was subjecting Gwin to this scrutiny as well.

He could take the abuse, the name-calling, the deafening whispers. To have her in the crosshairs was like death.

But Gwin didn't look crushed. She didn't look in the least bothered. Her blue eyes shone brightly with love.

"My heart is taken," she said. "I can't offer it up to

anyone else. Not my mind, my soul, or my body. This most honorable man has not only kept me safe, along with everyone in this town, he has kept his heart pure in hopes of one day handing it over to me. For a century we have lived our lives with our hearts encased in stone. Now, we have the freedom to walk in the light of day, and we're taking it."

Her words were to him, not to the rest of the crowd gathered. It was the bravest thing he'd ever seen anyone do. They could be rejected by all they loved and held dear with this declaration. Still, Gwin had chanced it. For him. Because she loved him and would no longer hide it.

Not for anything or anyone in the world.

Her eyes told him that he was worth it. That he was the most valuable, precious thing to her, and she would no longer hide it.

"Don't forget chastity," Lance said. "I have remained untouched and have not touched another in my pursuit of you. Since the day I met you."

Feminine gasps rose up amongst the crowd.

Lance turned to the Templars still sitting in the belly of the truck. "I'm sorry. I'm sorry we can't help you."

Sir Rex shook his head. "There is no need to

apologize. We would not have accepted the lady's offer to begin with. The vows of chivalry would've prohibited it. To sacrifice a lady for a knight? Not one of my men would've agreed to it."

Each man in the truck nodded, bowed his head, or placed his hand over his heart in assent.

"What will you do?" asked Gwin.

"We'll have to search for some other way to break the curse," said Rex.

"By finding your true loves?"

"If that is the way." Sir Rex looked off into the moonlight. "In the meantime, we'll be the guardians of Camelot at night and hold sentry around the place during the day."

The knights disembarked from the truck. As they did, the entire town rallied around them. Many young witches blushed and smiled shyly as they took in the new men to their town.

Attention was off Lance and Gwin. No one even noticed as they straggled behind the crowd. No one said a word as Lance tilted Gwin's head back and kissed her under the bright light of the moon.

"Get a room," called Percy.

Lance chuckled as he released his beloved's lips. "That's not a bad idea."

Gwin nodded as she looked up at him, love and

adoration clear in her gaze. "I'm ready to go home now."

They twined their fingers and walked towards the castle, their community, their home, their new lives together.

EPILOGUE

The room was in chaos. Papers were strewn over the desk. Clothes littered the floor. Books had fallen off the shelves.

Opening her eyes, Gwin's first instinct was to get up and bring order to her bedroom. That feeling passed quickly. She snuggled back under the covers and got closer to the warm body lying next to her in bed.

Lance rolled over onto his belly, taking some of the covers with him. Gwin didn't mind. It gave her the perfect opportunity to stare at his perfect ass up close.

"Ouch." Lance's voice was part squeal, part laugh. "What are you doing?"

"I was curious?" She prowled up to his chest and plopped herself down on his pecs.

"So you decided to take a bite out of my ass?"

She nodded, grinning too widely for her own good.

"That's fine by me," he said. "Just know that turnabout is fair play."

Gwin had no problem with Lance putting his mouth anywhere on her, anytime he wanted. They'd spent the last week together in utter bliss. They broke their time between the Lancelot wing and the Galahad wing, but mostly they wound up in her bedroom each night as it was closest and they couldn't always make it another flight up the grand stair.

Though they hadn't said their vows out loud to anyone else, most of the townsfolk accepted their union. In fact, the people were more excited about the double wedding that would be taking place. Nothing like a party to downplay a scandal and bring folks together.

Gwin was hesitant to go along with the idea, believing it would steal her sister's thunder. She should've known better. Morgan was all too happy to push the spotlight—and the responsibilities—off to her sister.

"I will happily nibble at your bits," said Lance. "But not now. We have work to do."

"Are you going to be like this for our whole lives?" Gwin flopped back on the bed. She'd become very lax in her daytime duties now that her nighttime was filled with so much sport. But her husband-to-be never allowed them to become too derelict in their duties.

Lance came over her, grinning down at her. "Say it again?"

"What?" She ran her fingers through his hair, watching the play of fire and gold in the morning light.

"*Our whole lives.*"

"We will be together for our whole lives." She pressed a kiss to his lips. "Nothing and no one will ever come between us again."

"You know those are famous last words of every horror movie," Lance groaned.

"But they're said at the end," Gwin countered. "This is our beginning."

"I waited forever for you. I'd do it again."

"Don't you dare. I want you now."

"You can have me tonight."

"This afternoon?"

"Just before dinner."

"Tea time?"

"Deal."

<hr>

Two hours after tea time, Gwin rushed to meet her sister at the LOC office. When Gwin arrived, five minutes late, she found Morgan leaning against the door with raised eyebrows.

"You missed a button," Morgan said.

Gwin fumbled with her blouse. But her cheeks didn't redden in the slightest, especially not when she looked at her sister whose hair was rumpled. Morgan's T-shirt, which was a depiction of one atom bemoaning the loss of an electron and the other atom asking if it was positive, was inside out.

"Looks like you got a little tied up," said Gwin.

"That was last night," Morgan cackled.

Gwin found herself giggling too. She'd never gabbed with the other married women of the town because she never had anything to contribute. Now that she did have stories to tell, she only wanted to share them with her sister. But right now, Gwin had something else to share. She placed a key in Morgan's hand.

"So, we're really doing this?" said Morgan.

"It's the right thing to do," said Gwin.

Morgan turned and fit the key into the lock of the closed door. The office of the LOC opened. Inside, the sisters were greeted with two desks. The ancient wood desk remained Gwin's. In the corner was a desk from IKEA that Arthur and Lance had taken a full day to put together, and that included a number of phone calls that resulted in Celtic and Scottish curses. But Morgan's desk was fully assembled in the new Ladies of the Castle Office.

With a little shove from Lance and a lot of cajoling from Arthur, the two sisters had decided to share the role of running the castle. That way, the burden was divided and easily conquered with two Galahad girls at the helm. The first order of business would be in planning their double wedding.

Gwin picked up her to do list. "The silverware has been ordered. They're using biodegradable cornstarch as you prefer. We just need to firm up the guest list."

Morgan nodded as she bounced on her balance ball office chair. Gwin knew her sister wasn't paying attention. Morgan held a book in her hand. Gwin noted it was Jacques de Molay's journal, the one that contained the Stone Templar's curse. Morgan had the page opened with the curse spelled out.

Gwin slammed the book shut and scooped it into her arms.

"Hey," Morgan protested, bouncing to her feet.

"This belongs in the vault." Gwin headed out of the office.

Morgan was fast on her trail. "I've never done dark magic before. What did it feel like when you turned Lance to stone? Did you feel your soul cloud over?"

Gwin turned to frown at her sister. "Sometimes, I worry about you."

Morgan shrugged as she fell into step beside Gwin. As the two made their way to the vault, Gwin peppered Morgan with more wedding details. But she knew Morgan wasn't listening. The only thing Morgan had planned with any detail was the negligee she'd be wearing on her wedding night and a Brazilian bikini wax appointment.

Gwin pulled her master key set from her chain. Morgan didn't have this set of keys, and with her sister's current lack of focus, Gwin doubted she'd ever create a spare set. As they entered the door of the vault, the creak of floorboards brought their chatter to a halt.

Tintagel was an old castle. It was also magical. Most importantly, it had been run by the most meticulous witch in the town for a century who ran a rigorous and thorough repair schedule. The floors did not creak on their own. Someone was here.

Before Gwin could call out, vines crept up through the floor. The stems wound themselves around Gwin and Morgan's legs and then encased their forearms. The witch fire that the two witches were able to conjure did nothing to the trailing plant. This was powerful magic, pure magic, fairy magic.

A hooded figure stepped into the scant light from the open doorway. The intruder removed the cloth from their face to reveal pale, lavender skin and flowing royal blue locks. She was the color of lilacs. The shift in the air brought her scent close to Gwin's nose. She smelled of roses.

Definitely fae. But what was a fairy doing in Camelot? What would make one breach the treaty between the realms?

"I mean you no harm, my ladies." Even her voice was musical.

"Who are you?" Gwin asked.

"You're going to find out very soon, and for that, I'm sorry."

"I know who you are," said Morgan. "Loren told

me about you. You're Enid, the fairy Geraint's been mooning over."

Enid's bright eyes perked up at the mention of Geraint's name, and then immediately clouded in shame. She looked down in her hand. Gwin couldn't tell what object she held.

"I'm not a thief," said Enid. "I will return this as soon as I save my husband."

"Husband?" said Gwin. "Who is your husband?"

Enid's throat worked around the answer to Gwin's question. She swallowed hard, her eyes glistened as she did so. She lifted her gaze to Gwin. Gwin's palms itched to heal the suffering she saw there.

"Geraint is our family," said Gwin. "If he's in danger, let us help you."

But Enid shook her head. She began to step back into the darkness. "I've done enough harm. I won't put any of his family in danger. I'll save his life, set him free, and send him back to you, even if it costs my own life."

And with that, Enid disappeared in a plume of violet dust.

"That's a neat trick," said Morgan.

Gwin looked at her sister. Enid's vines still

entwined them both. They looked like scarecrows with their arms held out to the sides.

"How are we gonna get out of this?" asked Morgan.

"What were you saying about being tied up last night?"

The story of how Geraint and Enid

got married,

fell in love,

and then saved each other

in that order

happens in *Arabian Knight*.

Want more from this world?

Be sure and check out the besties who started it all with

The Nia Rivers Adventures,

and The Misadventures of Loren

ABOUT THE AUTHOR

Lover of fairytales, folklore, and mythology, Ines Johnson spends her days reimagining the stories of old in a modern world. She writes books where damsels cause the distress, princesses wield swords, and moms save the world.

You can sign up for her mailing list and receive alerts and free reads at http://bit.ly/InesReaders.

www.ingramcontent.com/pod-product-compliance
Lightning Source LLC
Chambersburg PA
CBHW071230190726
48292CB00007B/2210